CLOUDLESS

CHRISTINE EVANS was born in London and grew up in Perth. Her award-winning plays have been produced in Australia, the US, Canada, England and Wales and are published by Samuel French and NoPassport Press. She lives in Washington, DC, where she is a faculty member of Georgetown University's Theater and Performance Studies program. *Cloudless* is her first novel. www.christine-evans-playwright.com

CLOUDLESS

CHRISTINE EVANS

UWA PUBLISHING

First published in 2015 by
UWA Publishing
Crawley, Western Australia 6009
www.uwap.uwa.edu.au

UWAP is an imprint of UWA Publishing
a division of The University of Western Australia

National Library of Australia
Cataloguing-in-Publication entry:
Evans, Christine Mary, author.
Cloudless / Christine Evans.
ISBN: 9781742587561 (paperback)
A823.010804

Cover photograph by Mathilde Delaunay
Typeset in Bembo by Lasertype
Printed by Lightning Source

This project has been assisted by the Australian Government through
the Australia Council, its arts funding and advisory body.

For Pat — finally

ONE

JACKIE

That summer in Perth
the city cooked for months
the sky burned white.

The kids were over at the pool
all day every day
baking brown in glitter-blue chlorine.

They had to take Jackie
whining for a Coke, for lip gloss—
dripping on their magazines
and stealing drags of Sophie's smokes
then coughing up her lungs
in front of everyone.

They could be mean
but Jude and Soph put up with her
because they had to—
Mum said they had to take her.

So they're at Beatty Park
all day every day
that rainless summer.

The complex takes a city block—
a chlorine palace filled with pools.
The long one's rimmed with stands
its racing lanes marked out
in black-snake shimmer lines.
The kids' pool's down the back
beside the kiosk selling chips and ice-cream
and, lastly, there's the diving pool
mapped out in squares of darkening blue so deep
you can't see the bottom
with five boards all stacked up

like in the Olympics—
the top is thirty feet.
Its tower casts shadows half a block.

That's where the girls bake
in coconut oil, on concrete
behind the highest board
with bloody cousin Billy bouncing round
in the background
like a caffeinated flea.

They're not supposed to go there
but it's the best place to sunbake
without boys doing bombies to annoy you
or little kids running through the towels—
and anyway the life guard's nodded off
behind his reflector sunnies.

And that day
against all the rules
a boy sits near them—
a shy boy (not one of those hairy screamers
that splashes in your face—
the Greek kids are the worst
then the Irish).

But this kid's not noisy
brown eyes, gold-brown tan
just starting to get muscles.

He says to Jackie, softly
I think you're beautiful
and the others look at her
and for the first time, see it's true.

Jackie scoffs and flips her curls
a little bothered, a little pleased
by the strange new feeling of being looked at.
A boy with brown eyes likes her,
yes her, *yes* a boy.

What's your name? he asks.
– *Jackie.*
– *Cool. I'm Karri.*
In the sticky silence
they both laugh, then look away.
The air between them shimmers.
Jackie traces fingers on her towel
(Karri puts his shades back on
but doesn't go away).

And the sun shines on her alone
in her tiny black bikini
with her don't-care Irish curls
and cat-green eyes
and leaves the others out
with their damp cozzies and soggy towels
and magazines
and who-needs-it-anyway smokes
and melting ice-creams.

Jackie basks
in the glare of her sisters' envy
doesn't see
the black snake nestled in their towels
wake up—
hidden by the stacks of magazines
and smokes and lollies
her sisters guard against all comers—
right next to the stairs to the highest diving board.

KEVIN

Kevin's eyes are tired from driving.
Stuck in traffic. Rush hour.
City summer afternoons are bad
And here's the worst part of the shift—
the bottleneck on Vincent Street.

At Beatty Park the bus fills up
with raucous flocks of pool-damp kids.
They flick their towels
and fight for seats
like greedy parrots swooping on a fig tree.
Won't get up for tired old ladies
so he stops and yells at them
Move down the back of the bus. Yeah, you.
No aircon—so the bus gets hot
and smells like dirty feet.

Back in the late seventies
when Bondy ruled the roost
(before he went to jail)
a craze for shiny glass hit Perth.
They stuck it in all the tall buildings
popping up like weeds in the CBD.
Mostly they used that one-way mirror stuff
with oil-slick rainbows at its edges.
Looks like mirror sunglasses for giants.

Gives you a headache when you're driving.
All you see's yourself
in window after window—
that, and other walls of windows
bouncing back and back and back
like glassy echoes in a cave.

They got that right, those fucken architects.
Now every east–west street's ablaze—
a howling corridor of light, come afternoon.

Kev wears cheap but sturdy sunnies, aviator glasses
bullshit name coz pilots just use radar
but the frames are light and that's what matters—
that, and bouncing back the glare
from crazy paving walls of light
that drive you up the wall all day.

And every building looks the same.
Shiny and hostile as a beetle.

City of light.
In 1962 they turned the lights on
so the space shuttle could see us wave
from space. First place you'd see
on your return. Last place
you'd see before the moon.

But on their return
the astronauts sailed straight past Perth
the city waiting, all lit up
with chips and dips
dressed up to party—
an outpost on the border of the void.

Perth.
The loneliest city in the world.

Seven years later, Kevin was in Grade Six.
Instead of doing maths
they watched the moon landing on the telly.
Slow metal insects stumbled
one by one

out of the space ship
on the moon
on a crackly black-and-white TV.

Then they jumped and it was beautiful
they didn't kick up dust—no atmosphere
just long slow flying leaps. If it was Kevin
he'd have jumped all day
played leapfrog with the other blokes in suits
then gone exploring—
but they didn't do that.

They just stuck a flagpole in a pile of rocks
and got back in the ship.
After coming all that way
that's all they did.

Kevin wanted to see moon rocks
and more jumping
and the dark side of the moon
but that was all they got
and anyway
it was sort of hard to see from down the back
with other kids' heads in the way
on a black-and-white TV
with bad reception.

You couldn't tell that much about the moon from there.

That night from out the back
the moon looked pretty much the same
though if he squinted
Kev thought he saw some tiny dents
from jumping astronauts.

He was glad he couldn't see the flag but,
because the moon was still his own
the one that shivered up the Swan in ripples
bright enough to read by,
made the dogs howl on a summer's night
and turned the shadows inky purple
making monsters out of jacaranda trees.

Traffic's jammed again. Rush-hour Friday.
Kev can't wait for sundown.
He takes his sunnies off and rubs his eyes—he's wrecked.
This shift's a bitch. The rowdy kids, the sun—
Along the Esplanade
the light beats off the river
breaking
like a bottle in your face.
But at last, the traffic moves.
Home stretch. He puts his shades on
jams the bus in gear.

Tonight they'll take the kids
go fishing off the jetty
if the moon's out soon enough.
After a bite and a beer or two—he'd kill
for a nice cold beer.

AUNTIE

Across the road from Beatty Park
on Vincent Street
in the brick house with the high walls
it's morning shift. Penny comes in
re-locks the door
and reads the refuge night book—
New arrivals.
Any attacks or threats.
No-one's up yet—good—she lights a smoke
and fortifies herself with coffee.
Once the kids get up, it's over—
best to take a moment while you can.

Auntie hears her, locks the bathroom door
for privacy, and has a little cry
then combs her thinning curls
and pulls herself together for the day
before Jerome wakes up.
It's hard being down here in the city
on a mission by herself
with Sally Jo's kid to look after
'specially the way they look at blackfellas here
even an old lady with respect back home—
an Auntie.

She's slow moving, a heavy lady
pushing through the city's shiny-bright
to find her niece, Jerome's mum Sally
tell her off, and drag her home
unless she's gone for good—
but that's a hole she won't trip into
so she moves slowly, carefully
even when she combs her hair
each stroke's an act of will.

She wears a flowing cotton dress from K-Mart
black flip-flops
Auntie clothes.

Back home in Geraldton, she works
in the sandwich shop
chops and slices all day out the back.
The young girls work the counter—
the blokes prefer that.
Baloney, white bread, spam, tomato
onion, cheese slices, hot dogs, rolls
with mustard, mayo
yellow chutney
bright green pickles
peanut butter
all sweet things that come in jars.

It's Geraldton. They don't wear those doctor's gloves
just to make sandwiches, but wash their hands
in the big ceramic sink out the back.
There's a fridge out there, and a big metal fan
but it's still stinking hot
out the back of the sandwich shop.

Cinderblock walls
a chopping island
trays of stuff beneath in ice
the stuff you put in sandwiches
by the fistful
till the vinegar stings your nails.
And the floor's hard on your feet for hours
because it's concrete
but it stays cool and it's easy to clean.
There's a grey bucket with metal rollers
for squeezing out the string mop.

It swishes on the floor like an octopus.
Sometimes it's the only sound you hear
at night when you shut up shop.

But down here in Perth, the traffic howls all day
rattling the windows of the refuge
on Vincent Street, across from Beatty Park
the giant swimming pool complex
north of the city.

She doesn't know this place
or anyone in Perth 'cept cousin Elsie and her mob.
Heard from Elsie you could stay
no questions asked—at least for long enough
to catch your breath—
until they need the beds for women fleeing men.
And Auntie's not in flight—
she's in pursuit.

Came down with the little fella on the bus.
We'll find your mum, she tells Jerome.
Four hundred K from Geraldton
red dirt town.
In the season, full of fishermen
hard drinkers, hard workers.
They make a ton of money off the boats
head back to Perth in the off-season.

In the season they work fourteen-hour days.
Sometimes they're out for weeks
way off the coast—
you can't see land—
out by the crayfish breeding grounds
the reef-rim round the Abrolhos Islands
where murder followed mutiny
when the Batavia ran aground

and, in shallow pools of blood and salt
and treason, hundreds drowned.

That's centuries ago
but way out there, time circles
like a shark around a bleeding fish.
Moaning voices thrash in the salty air
beaten by the wings of shrieking gulls.
Way out there
the wind and birds and water howl
and flicker like the static on a black-and-white TV—
unquiet, moving, meaning nothing
making shapes and sounds incessantly.
Only the sharks are quiet
and the killer waves
that rise beyond the reef to roll the boats.

When the fishermen get back to town they drink
and party hard, then drink again.
Blow the foam off the month's paychecks
that keep the sandwich shop afloat.
The money lasts them through the off-season.
It's a pretty good life.
The single blokes take off to Bali
or blow it all at Burswood.

The married fellas keep their wives
and double-garage houses
back in Perth, in cul-de-sacs
in Balga and in Joondalup
where sprinklers keep the lawns a neon green
and wives do all the cleaning.
And if the wives see other blokes
they never tell
and the fishermen don't either—
it stays in Perth or Geraldton—

what goes on in the fishing pubs
or the blackfella shacks on the edge of town
where some of them have girlfriends
and a place to crash when stoned.

They're not bad blokes
a whole lot better than the miners
who burn through town on the way up north.
They bring a bit of money
and fresh crayfish, that's a boon,
and lots of beer
and don't get into many fights
but the local girls—
the girls do what they like these days.

Sally Jo's the worst of all.
Since she lost her mum
that girl's gone off the rails.
Sleeps too little, laughs too much
smokes like cigarettes were air
and bourbon turned to water
glitters like a piece of broken glass
that sparkles in the eyes of men—
the fishing mob especially.

You just can't tell the girls what's what
though Auntie sees it every year—
they must know what they're in for but,
the fellas leave the end of season.

where you think they go, girl?
in the deep-freeze or what?
they got families you know

They hate hearing that word—
families.

BAT GIRL

Bat Girl likes the swimming pool in Perth—
a giant concrete echo chamber
walling in its sound-transmitting water.

Splashes, ripples, arrowheads of light
the crack of bodies slapping water
all form patterns she can measure
weave into a hard and shiny shape—
a beetle's shell to crawl inside and think.
A shelter from the world's chaotic waves.

Some are fast and violent, battering at her head—
the sound of human chatter, TV sportscasts
the flickered white of fence posts from the car.
Some so fragile butterflies could crush them—
whispering of light on summer leaves
the clink of sweaty coins in someone's pockets
seven aisles away in K-Mart.

Safe in Beatty Park's acoustic shell
she listens for the whistling curve of bodies
then the splash—computes the fall—
one point four three seconds—does the maths—
thirty two point eight feet high—that's tall!
Looks up, confirms. Yes, five boards stacked.
She hears the diver's shock-wave hit the pool-sides
not quite square—the sides hit first—
so roughly sixty feet across by seventy-six—
Good. That pool's mapped.

She's glad they've moved down South.
Less random noise. More bats
whose sonar patterns map the sky
in tandem with the stars—
a perfect site for building her machines.

Today, they're back in Perth just for the week
to finish business, sign off school, pack up the house
and say goodbye to Karri's friends
then hit the pool he loves for one last swim.
Beatty Park—*it could be worse*—
there aren't that many places all of them can stand.

Her mother Margie stretches out her legs.
She sports those cat's-eye sunnies
with a yellow fifties' bathing suit she picked up at the op shop.
Surveys the kid-jammed pool, decides against a dip—
probably full of chemicals and piss.
Margie'd rather head to Swanbourne
swim, then smoke a joint and drift with Jarrah
into salt-skin snoozing, after sand-dune pleasures…
but those sweet days went west with kids.

It's hard for her to set the rules—
she'd dimly thought of parenting like *hanging out*—
your kids your friends.
But Bat Girl soon put paid to that
and lately even Karri cringes—
hippie parents are the pits
Jarrah has a ponytail
Margie never shaves her legs.
And then there's Bat Girl, *worst of all…*
Karri keeps his distance these days—
just drops in to get supplies.

Oh—*here he comes.* Bat Girl points her brother out.
He's running, wet and shining from the pool
to burst their cone of silence—
Margie oiling up her legs, Jarrah rolling a smoke—
– *Mum—can I get chips and Coke?*
– *How much d'you need?* – *Five bucks.*

– Five bucks? You're kidding. Two!
– Mum…come on…there's other kids…
– Other 'kids'?

A pause. Then Karri shuffles.

Margie laughs *– You mean, a girl.*
Another pause *– I'll get you chips as well?*
– So, what's her name?
– Aww mum!!!
Jarrah laughs, but backs his son—
– Come on, lay off him, Margie.
– Please mum? I'll get Coke for Bat Girl—
Margie frowns *– I mean, for Beatrice.*

Bat Girl scowls, looks up. She hates that name—
it tethers her to some dream daughter Margie wants
who smiles, and likes to chat with her
and cares about her hair and what she wears
and isn't Bat Girl—
brooding purple flower in her swimsuit
sitting on her favorite orange towel
the innards of a radio spread out before her.

– Go away, she mutters.
– Thought you'd like a Coke, humphs Karri.
– Kids. Don't squabble. Here's five bucks, says Jarrah.
Karri grabs it—*Thanks, Dad!*—tears away.

His parents laugh, and talk in chalk-scrape chat
about *this girl he's met—I bet she's cute—*
the jangly noise of human back-and-forth.
Bat Girl presses on her ears and rocks—
her mother nudges at her dad—they stop—
the shell of splashy silence forms again.

The innards of the radio stop jiggling with her pulse
and settle down.
The pool's electric shiver-blue returns.

Bat Girl starts to work again, rewiring, building order
in a corner on a towel in Beatty Park
itself a concrete monster crouched inside
the roaring roads of Perth, a sanctuary from traffic
shielding patterns of its own—

Arcs of diving kids in glitter shields of spray
black-snake lap lines guiding swimmers
diving towers where Jackie and her sisters bake
and bicker, in the chaos Karri left—
a rudely switched-up pecking order.

Jackie's sisters' indignation raw and new
as if they'd never read a fairytale
or if they had, believed themselves immune.

At three o'clock, the sky is almost white
the sun consumes all trace of shade.
Sky and water bounce each other
light to light
and nothing breaks the lock of summer heat.
The sun's a ball flung high
a molten moment
weightless
at the apex of its flight—
the night too far away ever to fall.

SALLY JO

Pretty Sally, skinny as a cigarette
cheeky-smart, just turned fifteen.
Liked to smoke pot with the fishermen, flirt
show them she's got choices.
She didn't go with any of them yet
but Micko liked her quite a bit—
too much, thought Auntie.

Micko brought round smokes and beer
and showed her things like abalone pearl
and fishing maps
and how the fishing nets unfurled
and craypots trapped the crays.
He teased her about her homework
called her *brain-box*
told her stories about Perth
the land of sprinklers
the green city down South
except when she asked about his house
and he went kind of quiet.

You married then? she asked.
He answered, *No.*
But the chat stopped
the air went flat
they both took another swig of beer.

It was just them in the house.

Three more weeks of beer and crayfish
with vinegar and a little salt and pepper—
it was a good season that year
he helped with all her homework
and stayed polite to Auntie

who looked at him with slitted eyes
because she knew.

He went back home, of course
but after a few months
Sally couldn't go to back to school.

He did send cheques for the kid
and visit during the next few seasons
once or twice
but Sally Jo was finished.

It wasn't supposed to go this way
for Sally, smart-arse Sally,
the one kid still in school.
Sharp as a tack that kid
with As in maths and English—
that's trouble in a girl.

She was going to travel, work in the city
in a gym or maybe a boutique
and wear those little tight skirts and heels
and go out dancing with her friends
(she'd have friends)
and maybe they'd all save up
and backpack through Asia in a mob
and see Nepal and Bali.

Now she sits at home and drinks
screams at Jerome, who loves her
with the dumb helplessness
of a boot.

Sunny kid with his dad's blond curls
and mum's brown skin and laughter.

Auntie looks after him
gets him out of Sally's way
plays with him when she can
but she's tuckered out from ten-hour shifts
on her feet all day
at the sandwich shop
and all that time
every day
Jerome's at home with his mum
who's stewing in her lost future
and entertaining fishermen
but only if they bring her weed
or bourbon.

One day
Auntie comes home
And curled up in the corner
finds Jerome—he's cried himself to sleep.
Sally Jo's passed out again
with a bong knocked over on the floor.
Auntie picks the kid up, which she doesn't often do
(her back)
and sees his face is swollen salty
grey and black.

Auntie's brain breaks.
Drags Sally off the couch, down on the floor
and kicks her in the ribs
—*wake up you little bitch.*
Now Sally's on her feet, fists up screaming
Auntie's howling
holds Jerome out front—
look what you done, look what you done
you little bitch—

you're s'posed to be his mum
and all this time
the kid doesn't make a sound.

After a while of screaming face to face
they're swapping spit, so close
to hitting—out of breath—
it hits them—Jerome's silence—
and they stop.
Sally Jo looks at Jerome
looks right at him, really sees him.
The kid holds out his arms
she hugs him, close as a koala cub.
And then they turn their back on Auntie
like it was all her fault.

That was pretty much the end of it.

Sally Jo bathed Jerome that night
cooing over him in the sink
the kid's eyes never left her face—
he knew.

Auntie was just glad things were better
and Sally Jo had finally woken up
to what she had to do
now she's a mum—
but Jerome knew.

When Sally went to put him down
in the little cot in the lounge
he howled like a banshee and clung to her.
He never did that—
usually he'd go to bed for Auntie
after his mum passed out
he didn't even need the light on

but tonight
he clung to Sally Jo
and couldn't be prised off
without breaking his arm.
She probably considered it
but went to bed instead with him
all cuddled up beside her.

And silence curled around the house
like a snake in a patch of sun.

Auntie felt worried but couldn't name it—
her feet ached, she was all worn out—
fighting with Sally Jo no joke
finding Jerome that way was a shock
and once the fright wore off—
she was done in.
She went to sleep too.
Two hours before dawn the wind slithered in
through the drafty boards
wound across the floor
and stole away

and a black snake stirred
in the mud
far away
at the bottom of the Swan in Perth.

When Auntie got up she saw Jerome asleep
a peaceful, blissful sleep under the bruises
as if he'd finally got enough milk
his face filled up from the inside.
He was a chubby kid
but it was the look she'd seen on hungry ones
who'd had their first good feed in weeks.

But.
The room was neat, which it never was
the dresser bare
the wardrobe empty
just some metal hangers swinging
and Jerome's new high chair
with his clean shirts and undies
neatly stacked inside it—
Sally's scarlet scrunchie on the top
the one he liked to suck on
right beside the old tin bear
with all the fur worn off—
his special moon-bear.

No note.
No nothing.

Auntie breathed in the soft air
the sleeping boy
and paused—

knowing too well how trouble
sneaks in quietly
while everyone's asleep
so you may as well take one more breath—

before the kid wakes up
and you have to deal with everything again.

TWO

PENNY

Three a.m.
The breeze slips through the window bars
of the red-brick house on Vincent Street
where for once it's quiet
no-one's fighting
the kids have cried themselves to sleep.

It ruffles Penny's hair, then dies away—
a sudden chill in a warm night, gone
before she knows what woke her.
Now she's staring at the curtains
rustling, back-lit by shadows
flung by passing headlights.
Usually the glare of orange rims her sleep
(always fitful at the refuge)
from the sodium-vapour lights
that colour city blocks in shades of hell
but at 2 a.m. they shut them off
and Batman shapes cut out of bruises stalk the street
your eyes still full of orange sulphur
so everything looks purple in the after-burn.

Sleep's a thin and fragile veil on refuge nights—
it's only her first month of working here.
Penny's still figuring out the rules—
—*not that simple*—
everything's decided by consensus.
In a circle.
Every Friday.
It takes bloody hours.

Penny's hair's too long. Her voice too soft.
She's shunned the mullet cut
her co-workers all sport.
And she fears the *core collective* knows

she only took the job because she had to.
(Some evil snitch got her thrown off the dole
because she plays in bands—cash under the table.)
Her feminist commitment is in question—
she just might trade it in for male attention.

So Penny doesn't say a lot at meetings—
well-laid minefields lie in wait.
Even things you'd think were simple
(— *Can we get the freezer fixed?*) are not.
If she asks, there's usually a pause—then sighs—
then the patient explanations.
No men inside the house, for starters—
then discussion moves to patriarchal norms:
— *Why do so few women learn refrigerator repair?*
— *Should we work to get more women in the trades?*

So it's hard to know just what to do
on night shift on your own
if windows break, or kids run riot
or have an epileptic fit
or drug deals happen on the porch
or someone's homicidal husband does a drive-by.

Penny's anxious thoughts drift out the window
catch in branches, curl in leaves
and wait for 7 a.m.
when the kids will go ballistic till the TV's on—
relentless soundtrack of the refuge.
Though she hates the jangling noise
she knows the kids need something—anything—
that's still the same as home
since every other thing has gone.
The cereal is different, and the bowls
and brands of juice
and everyone hates the wholegrain bread

the refuge workers buy—
the mums and kids alike.
Kids aren't allowed outside without a worker
and their mums are sharing rooms with other mums.
And other kids can grab their toys
and everything just smells funny and feels wrong
in the brick house on Vincent Street
across from Beatty Park.

Penny pulls the sheet over her head.
Just three hours more.
Then after breakfast, Tina's on
and she'll go home.
Unlike the residents (thank God), she can.

JEROME

Headlights flicker past the curtains.
Auntie stirs, and tries to stay asleep.
But looking over, sees Jerome
remembers where she is
and feels her bones ache from the troubles
tomorrow's bound to bring.
She pushes them away for now—
their shadows flutter on the bedroom wall
like agitated birds.

Jerome hears Auntie stir, but doesn't move.
His toes are curled a certain way that keeps him safe.
He's learned to let his body lie
like Sally's T-shirt
carelessly tossed off, abandoned
in the rush to rip off clothes
when rising laughter and the low bass growl of men
with scent of weed, weave smoke-like in the room
and he's forgotten.

Jerome's skin aches for Sally in those times—
he's not the one she wants. She's gone
in spells of laughing longing, tangled in
with thicker sounds and smells
that frighten him. He knows
in moments when he hears the men
she'll hate him if he cries.
And so, he's learned to curl his toes
and make his eyes go out of focus
leave his body for the bird-world
tiptoe back when safe.

Now, in the strange dark house
where only Auntie smells of home
he lets his body lie

and glides up slowly with his breaths—
each one's a stair—
to climb above himself
and settle near the ceiling, watchful
waiting for the sound of wings.

Soon they come—a flickered shadow at the window.
There's the bird—at last.
Tap tap. Jerome taps back
then both of them look down
to see himself and Auntie in their beds.

The bird alights.
The branch outside the window bends.
Together boy and magpie guard the room.

His moon-bear's glowing on his pillow
pinky-purple in the orange street-lights—
secret anchor for his flights.
A silver cord connects him to the bear—
if he gets lost or drifts
too far away
the moon-bear calls him back.

It doesn't look like much—a ratty little toy
made out of tin, with glued-on fur worn off in spots
from where he's sucked on ears and paws.
Its patchy tin reflects the light.

Jerome's in love with tin and glass and mirrors—
magpie-glitter things that bounce the light
and (scarily) might break—
they sing the sparkle-song of Sally.

His mum's a wild careening comet—
swinging dizzily from laughs to tears

to stone-dark silence, then eruption.
On the good days, when she loves him
everything explodes with light.
Other days—but he forgets.

His dad Micko left the bear for him
one day he can't remember (he was very small).
Made mum cry—he does remember that—
she picked the bear up, held it tight
threw it hard against the wall, then cried
and picked it up again
and when he cried, picked him up too
and told the story of the moon-bear.
Best day ever—cuddled in with mum and bear
(it still had all its fur then).

This little bear, see? He's a moon-bear
got pale fur, not brown like other bears.
Moon-bear lived in outer space, his dad gone left him—
fucking prick—so lonely little fella bear.
Tried to climb back down to land
but always he got stuck half-way.
Had to climb back up.

One night but, the moon comes shining, sees the bear
gives him moonbeams he can slide down.
Whee! All the way to earth.

Bear gets happy, slides down moonbeams
plays all night with earth-bears
but he's gotta get back home
before the sun comes up
or he'll get stuck—that sun will cook him up
coz he's so pale like moonlight
coz him and loser dad, they come from outer space
some place the sun don't shine.

So moon-bear slides down moonbeams every night
and every dawn he climbs back up
till one night he forgot...too late...the sun come up
and moon-bear he got stuck...

She lights a smoke. And jabs the burned-down match-end
in the soft side of her wrist, her eyes gone dark again.

– What happens then?
– Oh I dunno. I lost the book.
She never finished stories.

The magpie taps the glass again—
Jerome drifts back
looks down—
Auntie, moon-bear, sleeping self—
yes, all still there.
The bird shifts, bobbing, on the branch
and violet shadows flicker through the room
as soft as blinks. Just eyelid-shadows
like the ones you see through eyes screwed shut
to block the orange sun.

On the long bus trip from Geraldton
those eyelid-shadows lulled him off to sleep—
a steady beat of bright and dark
as phone poles flickered past
their wires strung black with birds.
And lonely shacks with faded paint
and rusted broken tractors out the back
flicked past like dreams you couldn't catch.

The bus drove on, as Auntie dozed
Jerome sprawled out beside her.
Past flat brown fields with skinny sheep
and broken ring-barked trees

then blaring flags of used-car yards
and fast-food shops
and pool supplies
and cars and trucks and noise—
and finally, to Perth
and yet another big green bus
that brought them to the refuge.

And now they're here
and nothing moves
and Sally...
Mama can't be gone.
She can't.
She'll come and get him in the morning.

Night is grey and purple
and the branch is still. The bird is quiet.
Jerome breathes out, slides slowly down
rejoins his body in the bed
—a stretch, a sigh—
and sleeps.

The magpie on the branch
unblinking
doesn't move till dawn.

Across the river
in the backyard next to Kevin's neat box house
the neighbour's sheets and towels
slap
in the wind
like hard white hands.
The Hills Hoist groans and turns (it needs an oil).
Its wicked fitful squeak keeps Suze awake.

Kevin doesn't stir, though Suzie
lying tense beside him, wishes he'd wake up.
The longer driving shifts just wipe him out
especially in mid summer.
So after dinner, three beers later, belly full
he's pretty soon asleep when Suzie wants to chat—
it's lonely, stuck at home with pre school kids—
or stroll beside the Swan, and maybe sit out on the jetty
till the moon sets, then head home
not seeing how the mud stirs
and the water shivers
as the sleeping snake wakes up
beneath the river bed.

The night exhales.
Kev rolls over, quietens down.
Suzie cuddles up and spoons him.

Auntie's tired eyes fall shut
she can't do much but worry
till the morning.

Far away, an owl hoot rouses Sally
from her bourbon slumber near an open fire.
Her new bloke Billy's there beside her
still asleep, his shining Harley standing watch.
The sky is thick with stars, glimpsed
through the ghost gums.

Sally's heart beats faster
feels the hugeness of the night
she whispers *yes*, a fierce invocation—

wants to dance and hug the world
and rub her face in sky
taste the silver stars in tingles on her tongue
brush the black sky through her hair
and shake it round her face
shake the past away like water.

For the first time in three years
she feels alive again
and deadly.

PENNY

Friday stutters into gear
with spears of sun flung through the blinds.
Penny stumbles out, her hair awry
to face the morning frenzy.
TV's on
with blaring infomercials interspersed with sport—
the stench of burning toast
and unwashed kids
and half-smoked cigarettes
relit from last night's ashtrays
(it's two more days till pension)
fill the kitchen with a grey miasma—
a plastic bag around your head.

Auntie's up and trying to clean the kitchen
but she's losing—
mess expands behind her faster than she cleans.
On the couch, a woman's dozing.
Another's on the phone.
The third is rocking in the corner
out of meds—her daughter's coaxing her to eat
with expert, weary patience.
Three little kids are eating cornflakes cross-legged on the
    floor
in milky splotched abandon, after a banana fight.
No-one's crying; that's a plus.
Some other kids, the youngest toddlers, run around.

Big kid Darryl's tying on his skates
Jerome's beside him, fascinated
staring at the shiny wheels.

Darryl's thirteen at least—the oldest.
He knows he shouldn't skate inside
but no-one's going to stop him.

One of those kids like Sally, smart
and full of beans
and wicked handsome
plum-black skin, and deadly grin.
Charming as they come.

Darryl's always clowning, fooling,
no-one's seen him hit a kid or scowl or sulk.
He's the joker at the party—
lightning rod for tensions that push the other kids to walls
to bang their heads, or scream
or take it out on toddlers.

Only Auntie knows his secret—
late at night, when everyone's crashed out
he sneaks his schoolbooks to the kitchen table
poring over maths and science
grin wiped off like silly make-up.

There's a dog-eared piece of paper
Darryl pulls out every night—
a test with perfect score—his own—
hand-written comment *Excellent!* in red
across the bottom.
That teacher's gone, lost in the move
before the move before—
it's hard to keep ahead of Darryl's dad
so school's a fitful thing—
but Darryl has a plan.

He keeps it to himself—it's fragile—
other's disbelief would shred it.
Hard enough to struggle with his own.

He smoothes it out, his perfect score
his treasure map
and lays it on the table
night-face hard as granite, reading
squinting through the cross-hairs
to a distant moving target—
his own future
knows he only has one shot.

Auntie doesn't let him know she sees him.
In this place where few doors shut
you have to make them in your mind
and walk round other people's doors
invisible or not.

And so, she goes to bed herself when Darryl's in the
     kitchen
even though it's hard to sleep.
Has a life's respect for quiet—
who knows when it might repeat.

She has a way of drifting softly
into view, borne on the wake
of chaos, picking up behind the kids—
you never quite see Auntie
come or go.

Auntie's like a pencil drawing
half erased by many mornings
cleaning up the remnants of the night before—
like the morning shuddering the house today
behind the jarrah-framed
and triple-locked front door.

∞

After the banana's mostly scraped from off the floor
and Auntie's mopped it—
after Darryl's mum's gone back to bed
Penny's done the dishes
one mum's off to the DSS, another's gone to K-Mart
and the kids are settled by the telly watching the
        cartoons—
the house exhales, a leather sigh
and slumps back in its coma
knowing its own value—charmless,
dirty, but capacious
like a battered suitcase full of china
carried by a refugee
who left her passport, change of clothes
and every other useful thing
to cart instead this shattered treasure
to another morning
when the pieces will join up again
and make a real life.
Nothing really counts till then.

And so the house is harbour
to a world of washed-up elsewheres
and everything mundane collects
meanwhile, in piles, like dust
under the bed—ignored
because it's passing.

The laundry, shopping, home repairs
the broken toys and freezer full
of TV dinners—
these are mist, inconsequential
except to Penny and the other workers
who have to pay the bills, and keep
the cupboards stocked and stop

the kids from running wild, and deal
with all the chaos building up in waves
outside and in the red-brick house
which any day could wash away and lose its funding
or be breached by violent men
or stormed by cops.

A high-pitched shriek stops Penny thinking
of the things most likely to go wrong—
Grace has stuck a fork in Kylie's ear—
revenge for stealing Grace's cereal.
She grabs up Gracie
Auntie pincers from the left to rescue Kylie—
then the phone rings.

The red phone in the office—
the one you have to answer.

Cursing, Penny hands the kid to Auntie
dashes to the phone.
The news is dismal—Tina's got the mumps
and can't come in to work.
Can Penny cope the extra eight hours on her own?

There's no choice, really.
Penny wants to chuck the phone across the room
but locks the office door and thinks.
Gulps some water and some aspirin
then decides—
she'll take the kids and Auntie to the pool.

At least she'll tire them out
and get some sun
and give the house a break.

Now there's a thought—
You'd have to know the house quite well
to notice that it nodded.
Just a tiny shift in light
you might have thought a magpie caused
by landing on a branch
to shake the shiny leaves outside the window
and make the shadows tremble up and down
across the putty-coloured kitchen wall.

JACKIE

Three-thirty.
It's that time of afternoon
when sunburn starts to stretch the skin
and sun hits hard off walls of glass
and bounces off the blue
right in your face
until you find some shade.

The concrete slab
beside the highest diving board
is shaded by the stadium
after three o'clock.
The girls knew this
from months of research.

But that's the time the little kids come in too
the second shift
with shift-work mums
and tempers fray in sugar-fits
and Jude runs out of smokes.

Last year they'd just pack Jackie off
at three o'clock
back down the ladder to stock up
on Cokes and ice-creams
cigarettes and magazines
from the little shop
beside the screaming kids' pool.

But this year, she's a goddess
in a black bikini.
You know she'd just say no—
And brown-eyed boy would lift his chin
and back her up.

A conundrum. They want to keep their spot—
their towels won't do the trick alone—
but need their smokes and ice-cream.

Then like magic, Karri'd said – *Youze need a drink? I'm*
    headed for the shop.
They load him up with orders
wait and watch
until he's gone
then round on Jackie – *What the fuck*
you playing at? You think you're Lady Muck.
– *Shut up!*
– *Well you know what? You think you're so high up*
why don't you jump?
She laughs, *oh come on Jude*, but no
her sister's face is set.
They push her out across the line
where big kids wait to jump.

Maybe it's just to scare her,
just to show who's boss
and when she cries
they'll let her back in scorn
cut back to size.

But right on cue, the biggest boys line up behind her.
This is something new her sisters hadn't planned—
five hulking lads
and Jackie.
Now she has to jump.

It's thirty feet. It's much too far.
You really have to dive, not jump
or water up your nose can kill you.
One kid broke his back last year
shoved off the board.

They tightened up the rules
but now, as shadows fall across the pool
the life guard's still asleep.

Can't go forward, can't go back—
Jackie sits and rocks
pretending she's about to dive
and trying not to whimper.

Looks back, tries to catch her sister's eye
but all she sees is legs—
the muscled hairy legs of boys block her escape.
And Karri? Jackie shuts her eyes
and prays he'll come back soon,
and somehow save the day...

But down the ladder, running to the snack shop
Karri's run afoul of family. Just his luck.
His sister Bat Girl caught him, glancing up
from where she'd parked herself
encircled with her metal junk.
She spies him passing, points him out
and parents rope him in for questioning—
– *Where've you been? You having fun?*

The pool was his idea—
a last free day of bliss, while up in Perth
before they head back South to their new home
in Witchcliffe, far from Karri's friends.
Karri didn't want to move
but it's *best for Beatrice.*
Once they say that, there's no point—
Bat Girl's needs come first.
Today is all he got
a bargain struck with guilty parents—
compensation for the move.

He'd hoped they'd drop him off,
but no. His luck, again—
they all had to come too.

After questioning, he peels away
with promises of chips and Coke for Bat Girl.
Dashes to the shop
to face a queue that's ten kids long.
He fumes and fidgets
stokes the mantra that sustains him
—*it's not fair*—
And settles in to wait.

Meanwhile on the diving board
the boys are growing restless.
Any moment, they could turn—
Jackie tries telepathy.
Karri please oh please come back—
sisters, come on, get me out—
Jude is crying, Soph looks sick—
they can't do much to save her.
For there's a law the lined-up boys enforce—
ya walk out on the board, ya jump.
There's no way back.
No mercy if you chicken out.

Jackie Jackie don't look down—
that kid that broke his back last year?
he fainted when he did that—

The world spins round her, queasy-bright.
She sways—collects herself—
her heart thuds in her throat. She prays—
no matter what
don't let the boys smell fear.

PENNY

    – Sorry, but the pool is full, the Russian woman says
    her face a pitted moon with painted brows
    topped off by scarlet hair, sprayed solid in an up-do.
    From her tiny glass-shell office
    she guards the turnstile to the kingdom
    glimmering, half-deserted, past her shoulder
    the way a prison guard patrols a border.

    Penny, Darryl, little Gracie
    Kylie and the red-head twins
    are lining up with Auntie and Jerome
    to swim, with sticky clumps of ten-cent pieces
    clutched in hand, and three frayed towels to share.
    The kids are frantic with excitement
    Darryl's doing skate-loops around the lobby
    echoes crashing off the tiles and glass.

    – It looks half empty, Penny says. The woman
    lifts a bird's wing eyebrow
    looks
    too slowly
    up and down
    the line of rag-tag kids who range in hue
    from blue-black Darryl to the red-head twins
    but share a volume setting even when they're quiet—
    a brain-befuddling kind of thrum.
    They radiate a jangling chaos far beyond the powers
    of normal kids.

    Refuge kids, her chilly look says.
    Stares through Penny with a deadpan cold disdain—
    No deal. Penny's caught off guard; she turns
    but Auntie's suddenly in front.

Auntie's pretty much immune to scorn—
She knows that look—it slides right past
like summer flies that never stop their buzzing.
Always in the background, like the footy
on a match day turned down low.
Just a form of human weather that gets ugly now and then.

So Auntie puts her face into the booth
and says, real quiet
– *Be nice if they could have a swim.*
Don't want the kids to get upset.

Darryl sees the stand-off
doesn't have to hear to read the cue—
he howls and skate-walks off the wall
bouncing into Grace, who screams and hits a twin
who wallops Kylie, who in turn spits in his face—
till Auntie turns and bellows *STOP!*

An angel's quiet grips the children.
They all line up in seconds
staring towards the pool with fierce intent.

The ticket woman blinks, surveys the scene—
fleet-foot Darryl, followed by Jerome on stumpy legs
the twins; the warring girls now joined in greater cause.
And, rattled by the sudden quiet
she clicks the turnstile open
and the refuge kids rush in
trailed by Penny
still confused by what just happened
then by Auntie—
who allows herself a private grin.

∞

At ten to four
the light beats down
and bounces off the kids' pool
turning shadows into sharks.

There's a line of twenty kids
grown tired and whiny by the little shop
which just ran out of Coke and icy poles.
(Karri's nearly at the front—it took forever.)
Kylie and the twins line up, still scrapping—
twins as sunburned as their hair.

Penny didn't think to bring some sandwiches
or extra cash for snacks, but every time
she tries to take them home, they howl
– *Just one more swim!*
And now it's almost four o'clock, the time
when second-shift mums and their kids
fresh out of daycare storm the pool
and morning kids head home.

But still they're here, a multi headed beast
incapable of moving in the same direction
all at once.

Penny could have dragged them home
or packed them snacks
or never come to work—
(she thinks of these things later
weeks and months and years later
when it can't do any good)
but now—here in the blazing afternoon—
she's trapped.
Beatty Park's bright vortex melts her will.

JACKIE

Up above the kids' pool
the diving tower shadow's grown
to plunge the biggest pool in shade.
Jackie's stranded on the highest platform still—
it's been about a year—

At first she'd bought a little time
by slipping to the side—as if she knew her place—
to let the biggest boys dive first.
But then she missed her chance—
The boys' attention swung away
when some other girl's bikini top fell off
like hounds who'd sniffed new prey—
but as Jackie sidled back along the board
—*too slow*—they circled back.
She hates herself; she should have run
coz now—
her belly twists in wretched knots—
the boy-beast's massed behind her once again.
She calculates the shade—
—*'bout four o'clock*—
Karri—*oh please, God, come back...*
but Karri's stranded in the endless line
outside the kiosk by the kids' pool.

She waits. But no-one comes.
The sickening bright world spins on.
A mocking breeze picks up
plays with her curls, and whispers—*Jackie*
You'll always be alone.

JEROME

Bat Girl and her parents are still planted near the deep end
though they're wilting—
Margie's given up on getting Bat Girl in the pool
(she tried; her daughter howled)
and dozed off in the sun
while Jarrah reads the sports section.

Bat Girl's wondering what next—her revamped radio is
    done:
a lumpy metal snake spread out on a towel
resembling nothing ever sold in shops
or found in nature.
No-one stops to check it out.
And even if they did
her wary hunch and thunder-brow
and garish purple suit
would put them off.
Most kids steer clear of her repellent force.

But if they'd stopped to listen
even clod-eared kids would hear it:
eerie echoes of themselves coiled through its parts
compressed and high in pitch like cartoon chipmunks
mixed with splashing and the shriek of gulls.

Bat Girl's made an echo-capture trap
to amplify harmonics, re-mix them as *sodar*.
With greater reach, this thing could map out space
like dolphins do with sonar underwater—
an echo-sounder built to work in air.
But what it needs is power.

Bat Girl thinks of boosters. Cheap antennae.
How to amplify her sound-loops? Scans the scene—
perhaps there's metal she can scavenge from the bins.

Something draws her eye—a wink of light.
It flickers at the far end of the pool.
She's suddenly alert. *What is it?* Spies Jerome
—a little kid who's clutching something shiny—
Something pulsing with a sound-wave of its own.
Bat Girl squints her eyes—a sniper on the hunt—
and listens in.

Auntie sits with Penny, breathing in a moment's peace.
Jerome's on Auntie's lap, oblivious
to Bat Girl's laser focus
way across the light-lashed pool.
It's full of screaming kids that splosh between them
and the deep end—that's another universe.

He's transfixed by something else—
the slender figure on the highest diving board.
Is it mama? Is it her?
If he squints his eyes
and holds his breath
and doesn't cry
then she'll come back.
She will.

It's all his fault she left
coz he let Auntie see his bruises
though he promised not to tell—
– *It's a secret—only you and me, OK?*
his mama whispered – *OK, little bear?*
He's gone now. Rotten bloke. He won't be back.
– *OK mama*, Jerome whispered back.
And Sally grinned her wicked flashing smile
and hugged him. Heaven.
But he broke his promise. Auntie saw.
He'll never tell again—
I promise. Please come back.

But then a cloud blots out the sun—
the diving girl's in shade. And suddenly, he's sure.
It's her!
He clutches Auntie tighter
leaving tiny nail-moons in her flesh.
– *Auntie? Look, it's mama!* Jerome starts to say
but suddenly, it's bedlam.

There's a mini-riot at the shop—just run out of snacks—
the twins are screaming, pulling hair—
they'll get thrown out if they don't stop.
So Penny takes off at a run.
Auntie jerks awake, then shuts her eyes
and shuts the world out. *Just a little nap…*
She takes them when she can.

Jerome crawls off her lap. Then sidles, crabwise
towards the giant diving board, his head tipped up
to find the far-off girl—
he mustn't let her leave his sight.

Bat Girl's heart beats harder. Oh, she wants that shiny
      thing
the kid is carrying. And now he's on his own.
She checks her mum—asleep; her dad—engrossed;
and walks towards Jerome.

Meanwhile, Gracie slips, unnoticed, to the wading pool
and squats down in the shallows.
She's been holding on too long—
she'd begged the bigger kids to take her to the loo,
too shy to ask an adult now that Auntie's nodded off
and Penny's at the kiosk—
but they kept saying *later*.

Now it's later.
Now or never—Gracie has to poo.
She goes, and dances back, relieved
and joins the ice-cream line.

∞

By now, Jerome is almost past the kiosk
heading to the diving pool
but suddenly, there's something in his way.
Two moon-white tree-trunk legs.
He looks up—*What?* Bat Girl's staring down
but doesn't say a word.
Her solemn face is hard to read.
Black-brown eyes peer down through horn-rimmed
    glasses.
Furry eyebrows furrow in a frown, but not a cross one—
more like Auntie's doing-the-crossword face.
A pencil-chewing look.

– *Gimme that.* She's pointing to his moon-bear.
Jerome grips tighter, shakes his head. Bat Girl pauses.
– *Please*, she says, as if she's got a puzzle right.
– *Mine*, Jerome spits, bottom lip a-quiver.
– *Swap you?* Bat Girl digs inside her bumpy swimsuit bra
and pulls out coins, a shark's tooth, sparkplug,
pencil, three pink socks, a pack of screws…
she looks back up—too late—he's taken off!
– *Hey!* she yells—preparing for the chase—

But then a lifeguard gallops past—whistles, yelling, panic—
someone's shouting from the wading pool—
– *Disgusting! Who did this?*
(They've found it. Gracie's poo.)
Some kid's snotty mum, the kind
with year-round tan and huge designer sunnies

spied the evil lurking underwater
blew the whistle. Now the chain reaction—
first the lifeguard, face creased in disgust
then the woman who refused to let them in
her face a megaphone of *Told-you-so.*

More whistles blow. The kids are rounded up
and sharply marched outside, thrown out
while other kids are made to leave the pool—
Unsanitary conditions.

Auntie picks Jerome up – *Shhhh*, she says
not listening, though he's screaming *mama!*
I want mama! twisting back towards the pool.
This is war, no time for tears—
Tough luck, kid, you might as well learn now—
cut your losses and get out.
Retreating armies don't look back.

The local kids are nasty—all made worse
by running out of snacks.
They form a corridor of spiteful hissing insults
pushing at the refuge kids
who walk with stone set in their faces
—*shame job*—
looking straight ahead.

Only Darryl looks around and grins
his thoughts unreadable.
Karri, carting smokes and drinks
for Jackie and her sisters, watches gravely.
Knows the way a mob smells blood
from fighting for his sister after school.
Doesn't join in with the jeering.
When one kid gets rough and shoves at Gracie
Karri grabs him by the elbow

says, – *hey buster, that's enough.* Darryl sees
and drops his grin, and nods to him
as if to say, *when I grow up*
I'll take you off the list.
The rest can live in fear till then.
Karri nods to Darryl.
Looks him in the eye.

No-one saw the look they shared but them.
The blistered sun of four o'clock
bounced off the pool
then doubled back
to wipe the shadows from the scene
and turn the marching children into puppets.

And yet, some tiny hope was born
inside the public shame, some chink
that air might enter (if not now, the airless present
clanging shut, then twenty years later).

Sally felt it fifty miles away, a birdsong whisper
on her neck. She and Darryl hadn't met, but later—
decades later—
looking back, would recognise a fellow traveller
in the other, by the dirt under the nails
from scraping towards a future
only they believed in; gropingly, like trees
whose roots persist in salty sand
half-strangled in a taller forest.

But now, back in the telescoping present
fault lines radiating out
like cracks across a windscreen
towards a future no-one can escape—

back inside the red-brick house
across the roaring road from Beatty Park
Penny has a migraine
but the kids are bouncing back
and Auntie shrugs it off—so by the time
they're settled, eating snacks that Auntie makes
from sandwich fillings, just like in the shop
back home, they're laughing
sharing highlights, tales of daring—
forced march home forgotten, it's become
a great day out—
they want to go again tomorrow.

Penny shudders
and suggests the zoo instead.
Looks at her watch—five minutes more
till Deirdre comes
and she goes home to bed.

– *You look tuckered out*, says Auntie
grinning at her, asking her to see
today's debacle as a joke, a win—
coz after all, it took a while
for Beatty Park to boot them out—
they got to have their swim.
When all you got is borrowed time…
The key turns in the lock. It's Deirdre.
Penny jumps, and grabs her things.
Unchained, she turns to Auntie,
knows she's failed to grasp some vital thing
that Auntie tried to say.
But Penny's had it for the day.
She heads towards the door, past Darryl
tying on his skates and sizing up the hallway—
– *Bye kids, see you Friday.*
– *See ya*—Darryl lifts his chin—

She gives the twins a hurried kiss.
Jerome has quieted down.
He's in the corner tying knots around his bear
with Sally's scarlet scrunchie.
Last she sees him, he's a bent head
in the hallway, blond, intent—
doesn't kiss him in her hurry.
Never gets another chance.

Vision rainbowed by the migraine
all Penny wants is to lie down.
The dancing light refracts in shards
that break around Jerome—
and suddenly she's seeing double
boy on floor, and floating silver up above him
his reflection looking down
to see himself alone.

Penny sees, but doesn't see—she just can't deal—
so shuts the door behind her and goes home.
Ignores the nagging thought that she's forgotten
    something
some last check or safety lock—and anyway,
there's Deirdre. *She can cope.*
She can catch whatever she forgot.

Auntie lies down for a nap.
Deirdre makes a coffee, lights a smoke
and checks the day book—
New arrivals.
Any attacks or threats.

So no-one sees Jerome slip out
and find the open backyard gate—
the one that's always locked.

He heads towards the roaring road
that separates the refuge from the pool.

A little breeze, then quiet—
the open gate creaks to and fro
like an old man's fretful jaw
chewing on the memory of words
he should have said.

THREE

JACKIE

Four-fifteen.
Still stuck on the high board.
Sweaty, sick and clammy
hanging on by toenails.
Jackie shuts her eyes and swallows.
What to do? She can't stay here
she'll faint and fall
her palms are sticky wet.
She hugs the concrete helplessly
knees huddled to her chest.

She needs some more delaying moves
or soon, someone will guess—
she's never going to jump.
And—*nightmare*—half the footy team
has now lined up behind the other boys
to block the exit.
That's a beast she'd better not incite.
If they smell fear—

– *Hey Jude, d'ya get my smokes?* she calls
as if she's just forgotten
starts to crawl on back—
but no, the Simmons boy is blocking.
– *Chickening out?* he says, and jeers
and other boys start grinning too
the beast pricks up it ears.

– *Shut up you dick, she's done it lots.*
That's Billy, vampire flea—*good on you, Billy*—
– *Yeah, for real? Let's see.*
The Simmons boy smells blood.

Sophie, watching from their nest of towels
behind the board

tries to climb back down the stairs
to wake the guard
or call their mum—
but Simmons blocks her – *wait a mo—*
let's have some fun!
Let's watch your sister jump!

Jump. Jump. Jump. Jump.
Jump. Jump. Jump. Jump.
On and on and up and down
the boys are jumping, chanting so loud
the platform shakes.
Jackie wants to run.
She wants her mum.

She stands up stiff as staticky arm hair.
Stares at Simmons. No way out.
Bites her tongue hard. Metal mouth.
Jump. Jump. Jump. Jump.
Jump. Jump. Jump. Jump.
Jackie knows she's going to die
her only hope is not to fall apart.

Meanwhile—finally—Karri climbs back up
with smokes and drinks—
he's awestruck. Jackie's holding court
the footy team's all watching!
Sees his girl as goddess—
can't believe her nerve.

And seeing Karri's shining eyes—
Jackie yells out *stop!*
Surprised, they do, for just a sec.
She holds an arm out like the Queen
forbidding them to move
then turns her back

and walks three steps
and bounces twice
and lifts her arms
and soars into the blue.

A perfect arc
a falling star
a blaze of curls and limbs—

for just a moment
no-one breathes or moves.

She did it.

That's what mattered
entered legend
cleared the girls a space all summer—
Jackie on her concrete throne
her sisters fetching smokes.

Not the sweaty prior hour of terror
the spinning blue-white light
the fight back up from underwater
– *god, I'm drowning*—
towards the fast-receding surface.

Not the water, hard as glass
the sucker-punch, the bitten tongue
the visit to the doctor
and the perforated eardrum
not their screaming mum.

She only had to do it once
and now it's done
and everybody knows she can.

BAT GIRL

The diving tower shadow looms.
It's eaten all the sun—the kids' pool's now in shade.
Time to go home. Bat Girl's mob packs up.
It takes a while to round up Karri
Margie tracks him down—
he's wrapped around a skinny girl
who's shivering in a towel, grinning
both of them are laughing
like they won the Lotto
though the girl seems shaky.
Karri looks up, silently mouths *Please?*
Margie says – *Five minutes!*—and retreats.

Unhappy silence.
– *See ya Jackie. Gotta go.*
– *OK. See ya later.* Pause.
– *Bye.* And Karri peels away.
He doesn't talk the whole way home
consumed with what they didn't say.

Their car's a flatbed Holden truck—
it's done too many Ks to count.
It's useful as a workhorse
lugging Jarrah's building gear and carting junk.
It's practical for Bat Girl too—
she doesn't like the front—
the tin-can thunder hurts her ears.
So Margie and Karri squash along the bench seat
next to Jarrah.
Bat Girl bumps around the open tray.
She loves the roaring wind, and facing back
to watch the world slide past them in reverse.

And best of all—she doesn't have to talk.

She unrolls her orange towel, then—carefully—
lays out her rejigged sonar trap.
Sets the switch.
She'll catch the wind and traffic sounds
as the car speeds on towards home…

But not just yet. They idle in the rush-hour jam.
It's like that awkward moment at a party
when you've said goodbye
but haven't quite left yet—
hovering on the porch and making small talk
while someone goes to get the coats or snacks.
Stuck in neutral, idling
till the string of time pulls taut
and catches up the slack
to where your mind's already gone.

JEROME

Jerome hops, foot to foot—the pavement's hot—
with moon-bear clutched in hand.
He's squinting up through slanting sun
towards the far-off diving tower across the road.
A dancing shape—a silhouette—
– *it's her!*
He dashes out onto the road.
Never sees the bus.

Brakes scream. Burning darkness.
Shock unties him, cuts him loose—
Jerome spins out in space.
He rises up on waves of heat.
The black road shimmer-melt of tar
the glare of sun on windscreens
screams and throbbing sirens
all bounce him up towards the blue.

Soon, waves of splashing sounds wash in.
And looking down, there's Beatty Park
laid out in lozenges of light
three hard blue shiny patches—pools—
the long, the deep, the tiny.

The place seemed vast to him
before he rose above it.
The kids' pool, where they'd swum this afternoon
(until they got kicked out)
had seemed a world of bigger kids
and giant sudden splashing sounds
the deep end out of bounds.
Now it's midget-sized, and shrinking as he rises
up above the water palace
high above the highest throne
the concrete diving tower.

There she is! The girl stands on the diving board.
She's shaking like a fist—*you gunna make me?*
Like a cornered fighter, chin up, fiery.
Then she dances to the edge—
she's gone. *She's gone!*

He howls, but nothing sounds.
There's only diamond-broken water, sparkling
just like Sally on a good day
when she loves him.

He wants to stay—but shock-waves push him up.
He's never been this high before.
Way way above the pool
and screaming tyres and people
and the monster big green bus
and red-brick house
and messy road and sirens
stinking fumes
the tang of sweat on upper lips
and slap of feet—
a world all hard and clanging
like Sally Jo's alarm clock.

The one that ticked all night
and wound up with a key in back
(he loved that key
and often tried to suck it)
the one that Sally threw across the room
in punishment for ringing
and even then it didn't break
though Auntie said it would.

Jerome spins up through dancing cells of light
untethered from his body.
Grasping for an anchor, finds his moon-bear

clutches it so hard they meld—
at last, the whirling stops.

He's floating way above the earth—
the sky is blue-and-silver, pulsing light
that shimmers and re-forms like water
touched by wind.

Jerome looks out through button eyes stuck on with glue.
His ears are growing sharper, glowing
like the inside of a mouse's ear he saw once
when it crept into his cot.
Its ears were soft and furry, thin
and twitchy-quick and red inside.

He wasn't scared
but when he tried to pick it up
and put it in his mouth, it squeaked
and nipped. Then Auntie saw, and yelled
and chased it with a towel.
Jerome was sad to lose it
he was lonely.
Goodbye mouse.
Goodbye house.
Goodbye skates.
Goodbye clock.

Jerome picks up new sounds—
the fizz of light on air, a solar hum
the wind in trees and traffic pulse
the sticky city's heartbeat.
The muttered snarl of people's minds
stuck in their cars on Friday, jammed with static
He hates the sound of that—
he flicks it back with silver ears
that twitch like whiskers.

But then a tinny ringing starts. *Oh no.*
It's calling him to earth.
A tickling, buzzing, high-pitched pulse
mosquito-like, demands response—
he brushes at it—*go away*—
but with a thousand tiny jabs
it starts vibrating through his metal ears.

Jerome the moon-bear tumbles back to earth
and as he falls, feels gravity kick in—
he's plummeting back towards the road
where fear and chaos pushed him out.
Terror—he's not ready—where to land?
The hard black road comes rushing back again.
There's cars—he's going to hit—
then nothing. Darkness.

The moon-bear's crashed into a flat-back truck.
It rattles round the back, then bounces out
and skitters along Vincent Street.
Its button eyes are blank.

Jerome's in darkness—folded in the wings
of some strange waking sleep.
The dusk descends.
The traffic moves again.
The sounds and flickered pictures from outside
wash past
like television
someone's watching in another room.

BAT GIRL

Finally! The red truck heads down Vincent Street
past Beatty Park. But only Bat Girl's looking back.
So only Bat Girl sees the bus screech to a stop
as something silver flashes up—a star—
a spinning piece of light—it soars—
it seems to float—then suddenly it's falling
hurtling down towards her—*crash!*
The thing just missed her head!
It lands and bounces—hits her towel—
and wrecks her sonar trap.
Its shattered parts fly everywhere.
Oh no! That took six weeks!
And then the clattering thing escapes.

It bounces out of the truck and on the road
—*it's gone*—but then it rolls and stops.
Just three cars back. It glitters on the bitumen.
She scans—*do I have time? Could be*—
we've stopped again—caught in waves of chaos
surging up behind them. Piled-up cars.
Cacophony of brakes and horns.
The empty bus is skewed across two lanes.
A motorbike has hit a tree.
People—flashing lights—a siren—
Bat Girl blocks the sounds—*Yes*—if she's quick.
She hops out of the truck
runs back full gallop, grabs the silver thing
then dashes back and heaves back in—
Phew. No-one saw her in the rear-view mirror—
Jarrah's glaring straight ahead
(the road looks jammed for blocks)
and Margie's busy arguing with Karri.
She gulps some air, then checks her find out—
looks again. And can't believe her luck—
she's scored the shiny toy she hunted at the pool.

A rusty tin bear, fairly small
with nearly all the fur worn off—
that much she'd seen before.
It's humming quietly.

Bat Girl senses life—she feels its pulse in waves
so soft that only she would hear them.
Hopes it isn't broken.
But then the light shifts on its metal skin
and somehow Bat Girl knows—
the tin bear is in sleep mode.

She hugs herself and shivers.
Senses something vast unfurl like giant bat wings
in the dark, just out of earshot.

Ahead, the snarled-up cars start moving—
the truck drives on at last.

Bat Girl dreams of new machines.
A single star appears.
The jacaranda dusk pulsates with promise.

KEVIN

Friday just seems endless—
stretching like a rubber band from dawn till knock-off.
Rush-hour afternoon's the worst—
a sun-stabbed, sweaty crawl.
And everyone gets surly from waiting in the heat
—*the bloody bus is late again*—
like the traffic's all his fault.

Finally, just past Oxford Street, the traffic eases.
Kev steps on the gas to make up time
like a pony smelling oats
who wants to bolt for home.

It's just past five o'clock
when Kevin guns the 72
up Vincent Street, past Beatty Park.
He sees a child dart out
and hears a woman scream
as the kid vanishes beneath his wheels.

Pulls the bus over and throws up—
luckily there are only four passengers
and one of them is drunk
another two are kids
locked in an awkward kiss
(the boy has braces)
the last an old bloke with bottle-thick glasses
he barely registers the bump—
used to worse from the MTT.

Kevin gets out shakily
puts on the hazard lights
he needs to see the worst—
what's happened to the kid—
but not a trace—

there's nothing.
On the other side of the road though
there's a god-awful pile up
a Monaro hit the skids—
he must have seen the kid run out—
and hit a tree
and a bike piled into him
the rider's crouching by the road
trying to get his boot off, swearing
sweating through his ginger whiskers
leg's at a bad angle
good thing he's wearing leather.
His lady's sitting on the kerb
her head between her denim knees
she's probably in shock.

A girl runs up between the cars
straight past her—
scrambles up into a flat-back truck.

Sirens, cop cars, fire trucks, panic.
A screaming old black lady in a nightie
calling *baby baby Jerome baby*
had to be dragged inside the red-brick house
on Vincent Street—
an ash-faced girl ran out and got her.

When the paramedics came
she brought the old lady to the door
they had to treat her in the yard
no men in that house
no exceptions
one of those lezzo refuge joints.

Sedated, now she's back inside
but still no little boy.

Kevin radios for help.
Someone to drive the bus.

A shadow falls on Beatty Park
a silver cloud in the searing blue
a silver bear with open mouth
spins once, twice, once again
screams soundlessly
and vanishes.

Lost in the Perth December sky
where by rights no cloud should dim
the long long summer
where no rain falls
and at midday there's no shadow
kids are brown as beetles
and the lawns electric green
beneath the sprinklers
and no-one stays at work past five
and sorrow's held at bay
and half the men wear shorts to work
with socks and lace-up shoes.

It was Kev's last shift of the week too
he was looking forward to a pint or three
unsticking from the bus seat
and heading out to join his mates
after a nice cold shower.

But now—
after the cops and ambulances
after the sun's gone down
and all the kids have headed home
from Beatty Park
to dinner and TV—he sits and waits

for the back-up driver to show up
(he's got the shakes)
and drive his bloody bus back.

FOUR

AUNTIE

After the ambulance men left
after Deirdre locked the door
and everyone who could went home
a dreary purple silence rimmed the house
like tape around a crime scene.

Darryl and his mum have hit the road
ahead of trouble (cops are always bad
and now they'll swarm the house for weeks).
Kylie and the red-head twins were dumped in care
until their mother's Homeswest claim comes through
(fat chance—it's been three years and still they wait).
Everybody else is out beseeching rellies one more time
or headed back towards the men they've fled.

That leaves Auntie. In her nightie.
Dragged the jarrah chest of drawers
across the door that wouldn't lock—
it weighs a ton.
So now, she's barricaded in
and won't get out of bed.
Deirdre's knocked, and knocked again
begged and threatened—then gave up—
Wednesday's shift can cope.

Turns out no-one knows how Auntie got to Vincent Street.
One day, she just showed up from Geraldton
and started washing dishes like she lived there.
It was busy, kids were screaming—
by the time she'd finished
it seemed rude to ask—
so somehow, intake forms got skipped.
But now, detectives circle
sniffing round with nasty questions.
Who's this kid Jerome? Where is he?

Though there's witnesses who swear
he dived under the bus
he's vanished. Not a trace.
So searching could drag on for months—
the kid could have been snagged
and dragged for miles under a car.
Everything's a bloody mess—police report
with charges hovering, but what?
Negligence? Homicide? Child abuse?
Social Services creaking into action
refuge funders rumbling threats
TV stations drooling at the scent of blood.

So Auntie's left alone for now.
And finally it's quiet.
She's not a fool.
She knows it isn't going to last
so takes the breather while she can.
Staring at the ceiling from her narrow refuge bed
she doesn't move
except to track the shadows of the ceiling fan
with welling eyes
as if the fan could tell her where Jerome went.

Auntie waits
and listens
to the flickers
of the shadows
circling round the house.
Knows too well how broken lives return
as echoes
to the place that shook them loose.
Listens for Jerome. She half hears Sally—
then the roar of stars, and bats
and buses—static—none of it makes sense.

This far from home
she can't decode the signal in the noise.

Auntie blinks, and shakes her head.
Thinks that Sally must be close
—*them runaways all head for Perth*—
but just can't get her bearings in the city.
Doesn't trust the jewelled green of lawns
sustained by sprinklers in the rainless heat
the water sucked from buried aquifers
like blood from aching veins.

Back at home
a starker maths sustains her.
Red. Blue. Black. White.
You plant your feet
and every day's a fight to hold your ground
against the ceaseless whipping of the world
the wind's companion.

Primary colours paint the earth
and salt-tanged sky and red-dirt land
are mingled in the ever-beating wind.
A whirl with shrilling gulls, it never stops—
the constant grit gets in your eyes.
Back home, she squints and listens to the wind.
Its half-caught phrases sound like blurry tracks in sand—
tell you who's passed by
and who's passed on—
linking then and now in stories
told in dreams, or pictures
curled in wood-smoke round an open fire.

Scent of fat goanna roasting, happy murmurs,
everybody fed. *Bush tucker.*
Dogs like solid furry blankets

wedged between the campfire
and the night. Auntie drifts
and, back in childhood
sees her mother's feet splayed wide in sand
and hears her laugh
up in the sky
where adults loom
above the drowsy kids—
but though she longs to see her mother's face
can't find it— mum's too tall—
and though her throat's lit by the fire
—her head's flung back—
her face dissolves to black and spangled sky.

Auntie runs the scene again, just once
afraid to wear it threadbare.
Knows there's clues to Sally, and Jerome
if she could mend the ravelled rope
of past and future—
all the torn and broken threads between them.

Auntie shuts her eyes and swallows stone.
Hard to be the one to mind the kids
when you had to grow up on your own.

She'll have to stay and wait it out
till shapes and sounds take form
and tell her what to do. But one thing's plain—
she's had enough of people disappearing.
She won't go home
until she knows what's happened to Jerome.

SALLY JO

Three weeks on the road.
Her new bloke's nodded off beside the camp fire—
Sally's staring, sleepless, into red and ash.
She rolls a smoke and lights it off the coals.
The fire's gone out
but sweet scent lingers from the blackboy resin—
not supposed to call them that
they're *grass trees* now.
What's in a name—it smells the same
and burned with gum leaves
makes the sweetest smoke.
Faces, but—they're worse than names
you can't just wipe them out and start again.

On the road, her Billy's nice—
doesn't say much
never hits her.
When they're on their own
(the other bikies and their ladies nestled in)
he's gentle, once they've done it.
Strokes her hair and gives her cuddles.
Lots of blokes don't bother.

Sally used to hate that.
As a kid, alone at home
she'd work the mattress out the back
to get a cuddle. Got a few black eyes instead
for being cheeky—*asking for it*—
but the nice ones
they were worse than all the others.
Blokes like Micko—they got jealous
and before you knew it
everyone was yelling, bottles flying—
then the cops would show
and that was always bad.

Sally squints her eyes and dreams
of rice fields, smiling Bali boys
and yellow beaches, people
all mixed up together
no-one caring where you're from.

Sally dreams of India
and marble, and the brilliance of peacocks
strutting down the street.
And elephants
and saris
and those palm trees dripping coconuts
and monkeys dancing in the forest.
All the girls bejewelled and laughing
wooed by black-eyed boys.

She's seen these things in *National Geographic*.
Tore out pages at the doctor's
hid them in her shirt
and kept them private.

Sally gave the weary afternoons away
to streams of men back home
but no-one knew her thoughts—
or even wondered ('cept for Micko)
if she had them.

Sticks and stones…She's sliding sideways
wriggling free of names that chain her down.
Loose cotton shirts
and shiny skirts and skinny legs
declare her Indian.
Step by step, she's shedding skin
becoming who she really is
coz everyone says she looks it—Indian—

her grace, her flashing laugh
the fact she's clever—there's the proof.

On the road, it's what they say if anybody asks—
like if some bartender gets nosy at the pub
and fronts her boyfriend—
What ya doing with this Abo chick?
The magic words—*she's Indian*—make everything all right.
Then they can get a drink and have a meal in peace.

The whole thing started in the ladies
at a roadhouse just outside Kalgoorlie.
Sally's standing at the sink, washing hands
when a blonde chick joins her.
Sally sees her in the mirror—
hunches, keeps her head down, just in case
this chick gets nasty.
Then—surprise – *I like ya shirt!* the blonde chick says.
Ta, says Sally, off her game, surprised
that blondie's talking to her.
– *Where'd ya get it?*
– *Um, it's Indian.*
– *Cool! You're Indian? What's it like there?*
– *Oh, it's…yeah, it's beautiful.*
Blondie smiles, and Sally meets her eyes
in the battered roadhouse mirror.
Two travellers just chatting. Simple.

And just like that, she crosses over into mirror-Sally
the world her pearl, her flashing smile an asset—
not a sign of *being cheeky*.

Suddenly cut loose from everyday contempt
Sally laughs—a bird uncaged—and flies.

She stretches up—the fire's burned low—
to catch the starlight trickling through her fingers.
Feels it dancing on her skin—
the stars have thrown a party.
Milky Way, thick as its name
is spilling on the black and catching
in the branches, like a cry
sticks in your throat—*no use crying over*—

Sally's fingers turn to fists
and rub her eyes. *Soon*, she reckons.
Soon, she'll see Jerome again—he's better off
for now with Auntie. *She can get him fed
and cleaned up nice and put to bed.*

Suddenly, the wind picks up
and heat sears Sally's fingers
from her burned-down smoke.
She hugs her knees in to her chest
and in the same breath as Auntie
(far away in star-dim Perth
where orange lamps and headlights burn
instead of fire) whispers, *Jerome*.

KEVIN

Kevin's on night shift. His choice—
he's started getting migraines from the sun
or maybe it's from squinting too hard
trying to drive
with one foot on the brake
in case.
It's boring—night rides are all empty
'cept for drunks
and no-one's on the road but him
and carjackers and cops.

It also means he's never home for dinner
with the kids. Suze hates that.
But since he hit Jerome—
or hit the brakes and saw him disappear
he's been at arm's length with his own.
You'd think he'd go the other way
appreciate them more
but no, he's clammed right up
and shoves them all away.

Suze is worried, and she's angry
wishes he would talk
but blokes just don't, that's what they say
(collective wisdom found in *Women's Day*
is not much help right now).
She can't do much but wait
And let him drive all night
doze half the day
and try to get his head straight.

Straight lines. White lines. Yellow lines.
Double yellow, watch the curve—
the night roars past his windscreen
past the empty bus stops.
Puts his foot down on the freeway
speeding in the bus lane
which he never used to do.

On the shamrock interchange that feeds the Narrows
Kev slows down.
Glances up the cliff face, wonders about snakes
and the night view from Kings Park—
full moon over the Swan.

Last year they'd had a picnic
by the Pioneer Women's fountain
sloping green lawn, singing water
sweet as day the place—uncrowded.
Kev lies back to take a snooze
while the kids splash in the fountain
and Suzie reads the news.
And off he drifts
down sunlit waterways
the play
of river green on limestone in his eyelids
in his mind
in echo caves of childhood
splashing in the sun-striped shade
in mini-waterfalls he's made…

A sharp breath in, that's Suze—
he's wide awake, not moving
knows it's trouble from the sound.
Looks up, seeing nothing—
but her eyes are trained between his knees.

A coiling black snake three feet long
has crept in for a doze
beneath the log of Kev's left leg.
He sweats. He wants to laugh—that's wrong
but there it is. A snoozing snake.

She sees he's seen it, carefully gets up
to head the kids off, belting up the lawn
and calling – *Daddy! Look what I got!*

His quiet nap is frozen, now a Cold War stand off
with the snake.
He wants to run so badly but he can't
he has to wait
until it moves.

It could be years.
The bloody thing looks right at home in there
behind his hairy knee.

Who knew? The greenest park
the safest lawn to take the kids—
it's always mown
with gentle slopes and water games
and views out over the Swan
where black eels stir beneath the mud
and dolphins hunt
and sharks swim in occasionally
and jellies sting
and stonefish lurk
and no-one's seen a deadly snake
in a hundred fucking years.

Headlights break his reverie—
some hoon's forgot to dip his lights.
well, *two can play*—Kev flicks the switch

enjoys the speed of the response
the humble dip—King of the Road—
a bus's high-beam light's no joke
when blasted in your eyes.

That was fun. That woke him up.
He's speeding now—near 90 K
the freeway's black and empty now
2 a.m. and on the ramp
that leads to Canning Highway.

He should slow down
but senses something laughing at him
some black beast with yellow eyes
that lopes
beside the speeding bus
not even trying to keep up.

Kevin's belly twists.
He squints his eyes, then hits the gas.
He's pushing something vile away
some fucking evil thing that coils
and hides
inside the everyday—
you can't attack
you can't hit back
your enemy just melts away.

A hundred K. Hundred and ten—
he's pushing it hard as he can
– *Come on you bastard!* Kevin shouts
the bus is shaking now, the lights
zip by like blisters in a rash.
And then a dog runs out.

He sees the radiant flash of red
the eyes, the whipping turning head—
he hits the brakes and swerves the bus
it skids and nearly scissors—
metal shell is roaring, shaking
Kevin's pouring sweat but wrests it back—
it's swinging wildly
wants to buck across the double yellow line
and back—
Kev clamps the wheel, goes with the skid
tap, tap, release—the brakes respond
the bus slows down to ninety…eighty-five…
and then he's back on track.

The dog's run off in the dark behind him
never to come back.

Kev laughs, a shaky sort of laugh
that might turn weepy.
But he gets a grip. And slows right down
and lets the cool night air blow in the open window.
Feels it fan his face
and scents come back
and little sounds
he hadn't known he'd missed.

Crickets, night birds, quiet cries
the shivery paper sounds of leaves
stirred lightly by the wind.

The silver-blackened moonlit Swan—
that river's always there
close as his pulse—
full moon and plate-glass water.
It's bright enough to skate across
tonight. Moon-silver paper.

But then the wind stirs, water cracks
moon-silver alternates with black
and stairs appear that draw you down
through shifting waters
to the void
where snakes uncoil
and black dogs laugh
beneath the river bed.

Kev shakes it off. It's time for bed.

Suddenly, he's tired
but it's the good kind
the tired that leads to sleep.
He steers the bus into her bay—
he's right on time
hangs up his jacket, punches out
and calls the night a day.

FIVE

BAT GIRL

Bat Girl has a firm routine.
At ten a.m.
she goes downstairs
for breakfast, lessons, human speech.
At dinner time (six-thirty sharp)
she joins the others, eats her meal
says at least three things
and helps wash up.
She doesn't see the point
but that's the deal she's struck with Margie:
human schedules are the price
for Bat Girl's afternoons and nights—
she spends those in her room, inventing.
There's never enough time.

The daylight hours are deserts—
featureless and boring, hard to slog through.
Bat Girl craves the underworld of night
where bat caves join like giant cells
beneath the harsh and wrinkled skin of earth.
Free of people and their clatter
full of sound-transmitting lakes of water.
Bat Girl needs the quiet just to think
and water smoothes the edges of the echoes
jangling through the daylight world
and jamming up her brain.

She's dreamed of living in a cave when she grows up
or sooner—
if Margie keeps annoying her with schoolwork.

She knows a hidden world of caves is close—
she's heard it echo under Jewel Cave
down towards Augusta, south of Witchcliffe.

They visited last summer.
Climbed for miles down rock-hewn stairs
—*just one more flight*, she pressed, *one more*—
then further still they went
into the booming, empty belly of the world.
And in the echo-chamber of the earth
some tight-lashed thing inside her chest unwound.
The cave was huge, and—even full of tourists—
smelt of silence. Soft limestone and hard water
had turned the rock to million-year-old lace
and hollowed out the earth like honeycomb.

Karri loved the stalactites—
those dripping icicles of rock
that formed fantastic sculptures
drop by drop, over millennia:
– *It's an angel!* – *No, a cow.*
– *No, a stegosaurus in a funny hat!*
Bat Girl ignored all that.

Heard instead the whispered sound of water
—quiet water—miles below them.
In a giant chamber filled with rustling wings—
Bats. In massing numbers.
Bat Girl's skin formed gooseflesh.
Deep caves. And enormous.
And there's underwater lakes. Fresh water.
Home—that strange word—finally made sense.

My secret home—she rolls the thought around for months
a shiny stone she fondles in her pocket.
And now—*it's time.*

Since that day at Beatty Park
their house feels like a cage shrinking around her.

Three days ago
on the long drive home from Perth
she'd flown on roaring winds
as new designs for her machines lit up her mind
the tin bear in her lap.
Her thoughts stretched out and soared—wind, water, stars,
      bat sonar—
the patterns all connecting in some pulsing universal
      language
she could almost touch.

So, back inside, the shock of shrinking back to normal life
was just too much. When Margie started yanking at her
      hair
—like she's some chained-up dog to groom—
well, that was it. She snapped.
And Jarrah yelled.
Then all her brilliant designs were gone
slammed from her head by messy, angry, human sounds.

So now—it's time.
Sooner than she'd planned—
but how to map the caves, then find her entrance?
That's the hard part. That will take design—
she'll need a new machine.

Powering the machine's the tricky part—but now...
she shivers. Can't believe her luck.
It struck like lightning—brought the right conductor.
Something sentient made of metal.
A bridge between the bat world and the stars.

Her heart thuds, thinking of the metal bear
that fell into their truck—
it smashed her first machine and cleared the slate.
She'll start from the ground up.

She has a hunch the bear can channel sounds—
the sonar squeaks of bats
the blasting pulse of stars—
She'll build her new machine around its powers.
It'll send out echo-probing sonar
mapping caves through miles of earth
like ultrasound machines show bones inside a body.

Twenty years ahead of Google Earth
she's groping towards a universal code
that joins all things as information
turns them into powered pictures—
she senses it, like Franklin with his madman's kite—
a mighty force that no-one's harnessed.
And now she has the key.

But she has a problem—how to bring the bear inside
and, once it's in, to hide it in her room.
She's stashed it in the bush for now—
on the way back home from Perth
she'd tossed it in a ditch
so Margie wouldn't find it
once they hit the gravel road near home.
She marked it—*near that burned-out tree.*
Planned to go and get it later.

That's harder than it sounds.

For each time Bat Girl comes indoors
her mother checks her shoes, her clothes, her hair—
it's worse than going through security
at some bleak prison ringed with razor wire.

Margie hates to do it, but she's learned the hard way—
Bat Girl's collections can be lethal.
Black snakes, baby dugites, jars of spiders,

rusted razors, oleander sticks,
fireworks, matches, shards of metal—
her mother's had to confiscate them all.

So Bat Girl's had to scheme—no easy task—
to wiggle round her mother's strict controls.

Late that night, at bed time
Bat Girl sets her circuit-breaker on
to neutralise the house alarm.
She's going to sneak the tin bear home tonight
while everyone's asleep.
She doesn't often roam at night—
the sleepless nights unwire her brain
and if she doesn't talk next day
her mother goes ballistic.

Her parents know the only threat that really works
is human company
so if she breaks the rules and doesn't talk or eat
they take her shopping.
Agony. Half an hour in K-Mart
guarantees compliance for a week.

Bat Girl hoarded by the hour
the time she bought with good behaviour—
spent it in her room.

Tonight would be expensive.

One…two…three…four
Bat Girl lies in bed and counts her breaths.
The house is silent, everyone's asleep
beneath the brilliant silver river of the sky.

Tiny points of darkness cross it—
interrupted thoughts
so hard to catch; just flickers, really—
hard to see the bats.
She knows they're there, though
hears them squeaking—
sonar patterns match the stars.

Forty-seven seconds. Counting down now.
Bat Girl's mapped her secret circuit-breaker
to the house's grid. She has to wait
till it shuts off the trip-wire at her window.
Orion's Belt has one degree to move
until the stars and bats align—
so slow, the sky seems stuck, spray-painted—
splashy stars on black.

She's anxious for the tin bear.
It's been three days since she hid it in the ditch—
had to wait till now to go and get it.
Now she's got things ready—
she can keep it in the secret drawer she's built
beneath the bed.

She knows her circuit-breaker works
—she's done it several times—
but if she's caught, her prison will be locked
so, worried though she is, she waits it out.

They're hippies, so the house is self-sustaining—
solar-powered, not too hard to hack.
Her dad was glad she took an interest
helping him to build it.
He and Margie thought at first
the move had done her good—
the forest quiet, the huge unfolding sky.

And Karri too—a skinny boy, athletic,
running round outside
no longer fielding jeers about his sister
every day at school.
He'll find new friends, his parents tell each other.
He's an easy kid. Adaptable.

In the bush, the A-frame's built
the quiet clouds pass slow
the birds sing, water in the creek flows
wildflowers blossom
everything feels new.

Jarrah and Margie breathed out early—
rookie's error.
Saw the embers of each other
half-extinguished, come to life again.
And half in pain for what was lost
reached for each other in the night
their urgency all fumbles, out of practice.
Hoping this time
everything would be all right.

Jarrah's careful with his daughter
answers questions as they build the solar grid
doesn't overstep or chat—confines himself
to *pass the nails* and *hand me that.*
The fact she stays beside him
miracle enough.

Usually she bolted for her room
right after breakfast chores.
If forced to stay, then talking
often seemed a version
of an awful language lesson
where you learn to ask the time

and comment on the weather and the news
and ask about the family.

Bat Girl's capable of conversation—
doesn't see the point, that's all.
So working with her father, passing nails
and asking questions
seems incredible.
But once the solar grid is built
that door slams shut—false hope
she'd stay and talk to them at all.

Jarrah spent the next week breaking rocks
and weeding blackberries. Karri helped—
they barely spoke. It's hard
to hope. Then brush the hope away.
Hard to shift to something useful—tasks
that shape the days and later,
spark a gallows humour. Bat Girl's smarts,
her schemes to foil them
brilliant, worthy of the CIA.

Jarrah learns to laugh, and swallow salt
and work till bed-time brings exhaustion.
Margie lies awake and misses him
for weeks, until a glass of wine
(or three) at bedtime
helps her join him in oblivion.

Bat Girl's parents sleep and do not stir
and let the night wash through their bodies
with no residue of dreams
to weigh the day to come with omens.

This is good. They won't wake up
when Bat Girl shoves the window up
and jumps.

But in the next room, Karri vibrates
like a tightly strung guitar
that no-one hears.

*Five seconds…four…*a shadow forms
between the stars and window
shaped by flying bats. It funnels sounds
converting them to pulses.
The shadow's wingtip strokes the roof
the water tank, the drainpipe.
Finally hits the shut-off switch
beside the solar tank. And *bam!*
Her secret copper wires connect.
The winking red eye at her window
keeping her inside shuts off.
She pushes up the window
slides out to the drainpipe
slithers down, then jumps.
It's still 8 feet—no joke—
she lands with quite a thump
the backpack banging on her back.
That hurt.
She has to pause and catch her breath.

Unseen by Bat Girl
Karri watches from his window.
His sister stands, consults the sky
adjusts her pack—*hey, wait a minute!*
That's my Batman backpack!
Then she strides into the bush.

Karri fumes. *She took my stuff!*
And they're not allowed outside at night.
He counts to ten, then lightly shimmies out and follows.
No clear plan but tracking—
vengeance murkily in sight.

KARRI

After World War Two
the veterans came to claim the land.
An axe and acres given them
they wrecked their backs on giants—
karri trees as hard as iron
jarrah stands bled rust when cut
and stained their hands.

Those that persevered and cleared the forest
leaving bones of giant trees to burn
in scarry moonscape paddocks
found the land infertile, after all.

A bitter joke—ten thousand years of forest
gone, its sandy soil too thin for crops.
Its people dispossessed
yet Karri feels them watching
shot through the present
like the light on leaves that shimmers
when you turn your head—
just out of sight.

The moon's set.
Darkness feeds on darkness.
Somewhere close a creature screams its last.
Out beyond the mud that bears his footprints,
Karri shivers, curses. Lost,
he can't believe he didn't bring a flashlight.
Blames his sister for the rush—
he prides himself on bushcraft.

Karri thinks, then climbs the ridge
to clear his head, and see the sky.
But when he crests the hill
an inky tangle, black

on darker black, shot through
with silver, spreads out all around him
like a spider's web, with Karri
young and juicy bait
laid at its centre, trapped.

OK, you're freaking out.
Deep breaths—he's heard his dad say this
to Bat Girl, when she curls up, panting
sweating, too afraid to get up out of bed.
Five...four...three...
It helps. He's breathing slow.
No spider comes.
A breeze dispels the vision, shaking silver
into waving leaves. The web dissolves
and Karri laughs, then stops himself from crying.
Moon's gone down—no extra light
to help him get his bearings.
Stars don't help—their light vibrates and fizzes
conjures snakes and banshees
shakes the leaves.

Nights like this
you don't need Bat Girl's hearing.
Stars are bright and tritone sharp
their song a fizzing rush
head-splitting.
Overtones stack up and up
a dizzy grid that spins the earth
and sucks you into sky.

Karri doubles over. Needs Plan B
before the sky consumes him.

Suddenly, the wind is quiet
water whispers far below.

Or course! The creek. He'll follow that—
it winds back into town.
Shot like an arrow
Karri hurtles down the hill—
a crazy jagged path, pursued by giant spiders
and the laughing stars.

It's steep. He's sliding
leaping, running blind and yelling
faster faster, couldn't stop now if he tried
charged up on fear and speed
split-second dodging logs
and crawling things
and shadows—
till a rock comes out of nowhere—
Smash!
His knee hits
but his body spins, still flying
till a tree trunk, iron-hard
meets with his head.

Karri falls, collapsed, a kite
whose string is cut
his body slumped in soft-cloth piles
his mind cut loose and spinning.

Ten feet further down the hill
the creek winds on without him.

BAT GIRL

The moon has set. It's hard to see—
the stars are flinging greasy shadows at her feet
a milky, sliding mess of tree roots, rats and moss.
She jerks along
a cardboard box hugged tightly to her chest.
The tin bear's in it, probably awake
with all the bouncing. But she has to hurry.
It's a way to home—the window's hard to climb back into—
and her mother wakes, and checks
to make sure she's in bed by midnight—
the witching hour for Bat Girl.

Bat Girl's clumsy, never saw the point in sports
the uniforms, the yelling. All that sweat
and kids you didn't like with license
to throw balls at you
exulting when you missed. And teachers
with their whistles and their clipboards
creepy when they cared—it's just school sports—
and snappy when they didn't.
So running's not her forte.
She's a planner
and an engineer of big ideas.
Execution is an afterthought
a mop-up exercise.
It clears the surface of her brain
and gets it ready for the next invention.

But this? *What next?*
Success is messy.
Bat Girl needs a minion—thinks of Karri—
no, he's useless—
maybe she can build a robot for collections.
Send it out on nights like this.

Dammit! Bat Girl stumbles, almost falls.
The cardboard box she's brought starts squeaking.
Nearly home, she mutters, grasping
that she's got no plan—
how to fuel the tin bear
what to call it, where to hide it,
how to keep it oiled and working.

Bat Girl's good with rocks and shells
and train sets, watches, socks and charts
with everything that doesn't breathe
or need attention.

With living creatures, sad to say
the record's not so good. These days—
fourteen goldfish, several mice, a lizard
and two hamsters later—
Bat Girl's parents won't allow her pets.
They tend to die.

She isn't cruel. It's just their feeding
and their cleaning she forgets. She tries
but somehow can't decode the signals
others never have to think about—
the universal bond of creatures
skipped a piece of code
and left her out.

The tin bear's squeaking loudly.
Bat Girl stops
opens up the cardboard box and looks.
Its button eyes are glowing.
Bat Girl's pulse throbs. *I was right.*
This creature has a power source—
The box is filled with pale blue light.

Bat Girl smiles, then strangely, somehow
feels the tin bear smiling back.
Its eyes don't change—they're shiny black—
but something moves.
Electric moth wings touch her mind.
Excitement wakes—
the problem of success recedes—
the problem of decoding what connects them
lights her brain like sugar juice.

And in a blast of searing thought
she grasps
before she sees it
like a stroke of lightning yet to come—
she's got the elements she needs to bring her plan about.
She flashes on her broken old TV
(she scored it at the dump) wired up—
plugged in to streaming starlight
amplified by sonar pulses from the bats
channeled by the tin bear's sleeping power—
all aligning at the next eclipse—
Tomorrow night!

The eclipse will damp the moonlight
so the full-force song of stars can reach the earth
drawing colonies of bats.
Stars and bats will power her dream machine
to light the rivers underground
locate her cave—
and then she'll leave the human world to live there.

She sees these things join up with blinding force—
the darkened moon
then brilliant chilly light
the writhing wires

her mother's ashen face
night-forest lit like Christmas.

The tin bear starts to shake
its eyes locked on her face.
She shuts her eyes and slows the flow
then opens one eye slowly
sees the tin bear huddled in a corner of its box
and somehow knows
a thing she never knows—that it's afraid—
and strokes it with her finger.

Waves of soundless purring flow up through her hand
and twitch the corners of her mouth.
She's smiling. It is too—
though Bat Girl can't tell how she knows.
Odd. It's very odd, this feeling.
Later, in her room, she'll think it over
but for now—*fuck, ten o'clock!*
She shuts the lid and runs.

A sweaty hour later
The brightest stars have swung away
the Milky Way's ashy tail is coiled
above the A-frame
poised to sting.

A lumpy figure hides behind a tree
then dashes to the house
her backpack thumping on her back
a graceless robber, stealing time
in snorting gulps.
She huddles by the side wall of the laundry—

Crap! The window's shut!
Her secret entrance blocked.
Frantically she scans (the attic's high)
and all the doors are locked—
She'll have to risk the drainpipe.

Once she'd have shimmied up, no trouble
just like Karri—lithe and stringy kids.
But puberty intruded.
Now her hips have swollen
breasts are sprouting—
bothersome appendages that slow her down.

The star clock turns, inexorable
its lack of pity clears her mind.

She puts the tin bear's box down, grabs it
stuffs it in her pack, ignores its squeaking
clambers up—the drainpipe wobbles—
Bat Girl sweats and curses.
Several bolts pull out, a sound
like knuckles cracking—now it sways
precariously detached.
She bites her cheek
and leaps
and heaves across the sill.
The drainpipe wobbles...settles...
balanced by a hair
against the house.

Bat Girl collapses on her bed
her heart a thudding symphony
of stress and glee and almost-died—
cacophonies of blood
pound through her head.

The tin bear squeaks. And Bat Girl hears it
automatically gets up, despite the shakes
and lifts it out. She holds it in her hand
and feels it shiver. Button eyes are glued
to hers—which somehow calms her down.

Unreal. The girl whose lizard died
while hamsters squeaked in vain for food—
the girl that Margie couldn't leave to water plants
can somehow feel the tin bear
stroke its head and calm it down
and soothe herself.

A feedback loop that works—and with a creature!
Stars and sounds her usual looping-points.
Excitement floods her. *Proof*, she thinks—
the tin bear's made of metal
works on circuits audible to Bat Girl.
Now she knows. *It'll plug right in.*
And then—

Happy with her work, she crashes
tin bear tucked into the drawer
below the bed.
Stuttered visions
of the TV working
Margie singing, breakfast cooking
stars lit up like Ferris wheels
whirl through her head.

They sleep. The stinging tail of stars recedes
and dawn creeps in—
On Bat Girl, open mouth and out-flung arm.

On Karri, chilled beneath a tree
still lost in circling dreams of Perth.
(the hard-cut shade beneath the diving board
the moment Jackie turned and smiled).
On Sally, snoozing by the ashes of an open fire.
And Auntie, grey as dawn herself
and hoping not to wake to one more day of nothing
or for news you dread.
And Jackie, burrowed deep in dreams
of circling birds.
And Darryl, climbing in the window
of a temporary home
trying not to wake his mum.
And Kevin, humming to himself
the night shift done
and easing into bed to spoon with Suze.

Down in Freo, where the river meets the sea
Penny's conked out with another migraine.
The salt breeze whispers quietly
don't go back to work.
She won't.
She can't.
You're not cut out for it. Admit it.
Penny's hopeless at the refuge—
just a sponge that soaks up others' pain
and turns it into headaches of her own.
Shame and relief—
she's cracked a secret window
in a wall of *should*.
It opens in her sleep.
Her breathing deepens.

Penny dreams of floating in the ocean
looking down at brilliant yellow fish

in shoals that move together
like a single thought. They hover
turn as one, and vanish.

The soft salt breeze persists.

It creeps in with the dawn
to waken Margie, bring her to the door
and (seeing Bat Girl sleeping)
send her back to bed.

They sleep. The tin bear, Bat Girl,
Margie, Jarrah—usually he's up by now
and cooking breakfast. Whistling up the kids.

But somehow no-one stirs
while sun pokes through the mist
and trees
and through the open window
into Karri's room
which Margie didn't think to check—
her son sleeps like the dead.

Curtains flapping softly
in the morning wind, guitar left lying
on the empty unmade bed.

SIX

AUNTIE

Four o'clock. The slanting sun chills Auntie.
Perth's a glassy morgue of tunnels
blazing light at midday
freezing you in shadow by the afternoon.
The sea breeze hits
right when the office towers swallow sun.

Sleeping rough's no joke, hard on the bones
and sun on skin is chilled by stinging air.
She couch-surfed for a week, but Elsie's cousin
and her kids, and Jimmy on a bender
came to fill the Balga house
so bus shelters seem easier for now.

It's tough. She's lost the knack.
Back home, she has a house
and rellies (burden and a blessing)
friends, a boss who sighs but lets her go
when *sorry-business* calls (it does, too often).
Knowing no-one works as hard as Auntie
uncomplaining, standing up for ten-hour shifts
on greasy concrete floors.

It's only for a bit, she tells herself. The refuge closed
and all the women had to leave. It's *in review*—
bad-sounding phrase—what happened with Jerome
has blown the lid. Drug dealing, minors, prostitutes—
the snoops are nosing round with licking lips
to wipe the refuge off the map
and send the women back to men
who beat them
in the suburbs, where it's quiet.

In Auntie's world, when uniforms step in
it's time to disappear—
they have a way of wrecking things that balance by a hair.
And then the kids are gone.

She should go home. She can't. (Jerome.)
And Sally's nowhere to be found—she's asked.
That girl's gone off the map.

Auntie's waiting, but unravels.
Feels the life drain through her skin
the kids dispersed—
first Sally, then Jerome—
although she tried so hard to hold them in.
At times she feels a cracking in her chest
the splintered tree of family her ribs.

In Perth, she's at a loss for where to look.
And people look straight through her
rushing home from work—
an old black lady at the bus stop
something that the wind blew in, left-over
with the cans and papers.
Human litter.

And it's not her country—nothing sings.
Though she watches birds and buses
light on water, clouds and lizards
nothing comes in focus.
Where you gone, Jerome? She has to know.
The howling wind plays dumb.

Five o'clock. The cop car, cruising,
passes Auntie for the second time—
she'd better move along. Carefully
she fondles her last card. A bus pass.

Penny gave it to her when she left—
couldn't talk for tears, the silly girl—
Walking bruise, thinks Auntie, *that one,*
soft as butter—never got why Penny works the refuge—
hasn't she got family of her own?

The bus pass though—that's useful.
And here's the 72. Right in the nick of time.
So on she gets (before the cop car circles back)
to prove she's going somewhere
like the rest of Perth in rush hour.

Auntie's slow to board (her knees).
So in the rear-view mirror
Kevin watches, waits for her to sit
before he slips the clutch
and starts the long last leg
(he hates this shift)
beside the beaten-metal river
down the sun-speared Esplanade
where traffic crawls like beetles on his skin,
and night, in hiding from the glare
might never fall.

They circle past the Narrows
through that bloody bottleneck
and cross the bridge to Applecross.

Jackie, pool-damp goddess, tanned
and flanked by fans and sisters
shoves her way on board at Vincent Street
ahead of all the other kids.
(In the mirror, safe behind reflector glasses
Kevin tracks her little bottom swinging down the bus
to claim the back seat with the rowdy boys.)

The bus is jammed. Office workers, teens
and mums weighed down with shopping
bang into kids' backpacks, toddlers whining—
sprawling school-kids claim the seats
despite the shoppers' glares.
Sweaty men in polyester shirts stick to the hand-straps
jackets open, panting.
Slowly, as the sun concedes the sky
the bus disgorges people, sighing in relief
each time it stops and spills a few more bodies
gulps in some new air.

Now they're on the home stretch.
Bus is almost empty.
Jackie and her entourage
like a cloud of screeching lorikeets
take off, and suddenly it's quiet.
Sky is softening—
cirrus clouds are edged with pink and gold.
Kev breathes out, and cracks his neck
adjusts his sunnies—checks the mirror.
Auntie's up the back, unmoving
stone-carved in her plastic seat.
Medusa of the Buses—
staring straight ahead.

Kevin freezes. Doesn't know what chills him.
Why the sight of Auntie
down and out but harmless
makes his hands shake on the wheel.
She should have got off stops ago—
they're circling back past Perth—but no.
And just like that, with loping ease
beside the bus, the black dog's back.
Invisible to everyone but Kevin.

Kevin locks his jaw and locks the wheel
and drives on willpower, looking straight ahead.
But straight ahead's a tricky thing with buses.
Trains, perhaps—but buses circle
though it doesn't seem that way unless you drive.
Kevin's job's the ticking second hand
that crawls the minutes on the clock
and after circling, turns again.
Right back to where you started.

Like the junk that's left in space
to circle round the moon.

But passengers can move in lines—
they're going somewhere after all.
Where's this one headed?
Round and round with Kevin
and the dog beside the bus.
The three of them ensnared
inside a wind-up metal watch
with no escape. His heart thumps.
Hands are sweating. Trapped.

Time crumples and expands
his bus a broken beetle, stranded
Auntie frozen in the back.

He grinds the gears and pulls the bus up
in between stops—never does that—
looks back in the mirror. Auntie
doesn't move a hair. They stare
like that, with Kevin looking back
and Auntie frozen. *What's she thinking?*

– *How you going, love? You lost?* he asks.
But Auntie doesn't answer.

Now she's closed her eyes—too late—
deciding to play mum.
Kevin's jitters turn to anger. Needs to act.
He strides down to the back. Then, loudly
– *Wake up, love. You lost?*
Auntie squints. Says nothing.
Where you going? Kevin tries again.
Another pause. Then – *Home,* says Auntie.
– *Home,* says Kevin. *Right. Where's that?*
But Auntie doesn't answer.
You can't stay on the bus all night, says Kev.
So, where's your stop? She pauses, thinks,
pulls out a name: – *On Vincent Street.*
– *You've missed it then. That's ten blocks back.*
– *Oh well. I'll get off next time round.* she says—
she's called his bluff.

It's up to Kevin now to chuck her off
or drive the three-hour loop again with Auntie
sending ice cubes down his neck.
He's had enough. *All right then—*
gearing up—but then he stops.
She's looking at him.

Kevin's seen that look before
in creatures by the road hit by a car
who know they can't escape
as you approach, but try
to raise their head
and look you in the eye
and hold their ground
and hope you go away.

– *Sit tight, love,* Kevin says instead, surprised
to hear the words come out.
We'll get you home.

It's long, but. Might be quicker walking—
but she's bunkered in and closed her eyes—
short of dynamite, Auntie isn't budging.

Kevin starts back up.
And feels a fool, coz everything seems normal—
black dog's gone—old lady down the back, asleep.
He shakes his head and rolls his shoulders
wondering what spooked him—
can't recall now.
Puts it down to too much overtime this week.

The bus moves steady through the twilight
circling river, city, park. The streetlights cast
their weak illumination, barely present—
Lit too early to dispel the dark.

SALLY JO

Motorbikes are cool, but days of dead flat road
don't give you much to look at.
Red dirt. Scrub. The Nullarbor horizon.
Billy's beefy back in denim cling wrap
sweating in your face.
And your bum gets sore from sitting hours on end.
Can't even walk around or talk.

She's glad that's past—they've made it over East.

It's sunset at some weathered Queensland pub
where crimson bougainvillea climbs the walls
and flocks of parrots squawk in giant trees.
The bikes are parked in shining rows.
The other chicks are getting jugs of beer—
for now, it's only Sally and the blokes.
Ignoring her, they're cracking jokes and drooling
planning their next stop. There's rumours—
music, drugs on tap, mud-wrestling—
hippie chicks are easy meat—
they'll rip through Maleny's folk festival
like dingoes through a backyard full of chooks.

Sally laughs, but not that loud.
The cage around her thoughts slams shut.
She pours another beer and lights a smoke.
The jukebox flips another song—
The Harder They Come.
Frangipani scent and jasmine mix with frying meat.

Sally's cigarette smoke twines in drifting spirals
circling dreams of freedom like a hawk
who floats with no apparent aim
until it spies its prey—then dives.

She squints her eyes, makes eyelash-prism rainbows
lets the voices fade, and sways
in colour to a reggae beat.
Feels through half-shut eyes the world—
it's waiting—somewhere—singing to her
pulsing through some wall that's paper thin—

And right then, like she'd willed it to the carpark
a battered once-white Kombi van pulls in.

She watches them get out with narrowed eyes.
Two tall thin blokes in rolled-up pants. A skinny girl
about her age, a dirty blonde, with wild and matted hair
and purple skirt. Two other plumper girls,
one dark-haired, the other blazing red, her face so pale
it's like the surface of the moon
beneath the sumptuous scarlet of her head.
They don't add up. Not couples—*family? A tribe?*
No spare blokes—*a pity.* That door's shut.

They straggle in like some strange flock of birds.
Check out the bikies with a hurried glance
then take the farthest wooden table from them
buffered by some old blokes in between—
they're playing poker, sitting round a jug of beer
while wives in faded cardigans yarn on—
The price of milk. The weevils in the flour.
The rotten peanut crop this season.

Sally's beer goes flat. She waits.
The sun crawls down the sky, so slow
it could be painted on some lurid motel wall—
a tropic scene, forever afternoon—
the colours far too bright for real life. But finally
the sun sets. Hammered, Sally's crew rolls out
to set up camp. – *You comin', Sal?* says Bill.

– Be right there. Finishing up my beer.
– OK. He stumbles off.

Sally puts her untouched beer down.
Stubs her smoke out.
This is it. *The world.* Her chance—
She steadies—feeling sick—then saunters over
hopes that they won't hear her thudding heart.

Five strange pairs of eyes turn up and stare.
– Hey there, Sally says. *So how's it going?*
Where youze headed?
Silence.
Sally swallows, braces
for the lizard-eye quick flicker that she dreads
the double-take—
but—*phew*—she passes.

The moon-faced redhead smiles.
– Going to Maleny. How 'bout you?
– No shit? Amazing! Wow. I'm going there too!
Sally's smile is dazzling.

Late next morning, on the highway north
the Kombi chugs along. Sally's in the front.
She's singing with her new best friends—
they're in a band—original folk-rock—The Elves.
And Janie's matted hair is *Celtic elf-locks*—
tribal from her Irish roots—not dreads.
Sally's never heard of Celts, but doesn't miss a beat
– I'm Indian meself.
– Deadset? A gypsy?
– What? I guess. Yeah, probably.
– They come from India, you know. The Romany.

— The what?
— The gypsies! They're your tribe!
And Sally beams.

The world spins on and on in colours, flung
by crystals hanging in the window.
Woven rainbows fill the van.
Sally laughs and sings.
Never glances in the rear-view mirror—
nothing there to see but empty road.
In any case, they're hours ahead—
she'd never spot the bloke she shed this morning
like a cast-off skin—
snuck out at dawn
no note—
no nothing—
stuff like that, it's best to do it clean.

Bob Marley rocks the kombi onwards
Janie lights another joint. *— Can you sing back-up?*
— Sure, says Sally. *— With the band?*
— Of course. She takes another toke
and flings her heart into the future, sings along—
she's almost learned this one.

Hasn't learned the heart's a boomerang—
the harder flung, the harder it returns.

JACKIE

Night in Perth. The swimming pool's deserted.
Sheets of water lie in sunless silence, clear as glass.
The pool seems empty, drained of water
filled with air. But nothing stirs—no breeze.

Curls stuck to her forehead
Jackie tosses in the sweaty night. Can't quite wake
but fretfully asleep, she's swimming up
through miles of water
bubbles leading to the light
though she's kicking hard, and rising
the surface is receding faster, silvered over
trapping her beneath its one-way mirror.

She hears her sisters laughing far away.
They're heading home.
And Karri's gone.
He's never coming back.
She's all alone.
They're leaving her to drown.
Her bitten tongue tastes salt.
She struggles—
then a tapping wakes her.
Jackie heaves in air—
she's shaking—then sits up—what *was* that?

There it is again—a far-off rattle and a swooshing sound.
A wing-shaped shadow strokes the window.
Jackie leaves her bed and looks outside.
At first, her sleep-blurred eyes see nothing.
Then a figure, dark on dark, takes shape
circling in the empty carpark by the swimming pool.

Jackie watches. In the quiet between dream and dawn
it glides around in circles, black and silver

like a bird in human form.
Light glints from its heels—does it have wings
like—*what's that god*—the messenger?

Jackie feels her breath return
as if the figure danced the breeze back just for her.
She watches for a while.
The circling rhythm calms her down
till tiredness pulls her, yawning, back to bed.

Beatty Park is quiet. The breeze stirs
sketching tiny wrinkles on the water, barely there
before they're gone.

A streetlight shines on bits of broken glass.

In the empty carpark, Darryl skates.
Soon, he'll have to crawl back in the window
of this week's airless cage—cousin Ronnie's flat—
before his mum wakes up—
soon—but not quite yet. *Come on*—

He circles, bends his knees and speeds
feels the world roar past—he's almost there—
almost fast enough to melt its shell
and blur it into nothing
step right through and out the other side
to some place he can breathe—
he's close—but not quite close enough.
His muscles strain. He's panting. Falling—
Lands back in the lightless concrete void.

Darryl's skates flash silver, circling in the darkness
glinting and then gone
like a dream you can't remember.

SEVEN

BAT GIRL

Sunlight stabs her eyes.
The morning cracks in shards of white.
Margie's shaking Bat Girl
shouting, breaking all their careful rules,
—the knock, the pause—
the space she needs to don her diving suit
and enter human voices slowly
like a swimmer in a raging sea.

Bat Girl shrieks and dives for cover
Margie doesn't stop.
– *Get up, Missy! Cut the bullshit.*
Where's your brother?
Bat Girl plugs her ear and whines
huddles in the fleeing dark. No deal.
Jarrah's in the room
to tear the sheets back, throw them out the door.
– *Get up RIGHT NOW!* he bellows.
Shocked, she sits straight up and looks him in the eye.
A moment's pause—she never does this
pay attention on demand—
Margie blinks, and files the incident
for later, under *progress*. Now, however—

– *Karri's gone*, her dad says, capturing her hands.
So—Where'd he go? We have to know.
– *We know you shimmied out last night*—that's Margie—
– *Didn't!* spits out Bat Girl.
– *Liar!* snaps her mother back.
Look at the floor! Bat Girl looks—she's caught.
There's mud and leaves and, worst of all
her brother's backpack
half-unzipped and spilling on the floor.

– How could you! screams her mother.
Bat Girl whimpers
feels the words as bricks thrown at her head.
She rocks again.
– Listen honey—that's her dad.
He's learned to tamp down higher overtones
Mum and me aren't angry. (Margie rolls her eyes.)
We just need information. Bat Girl calms a little.
Where and when. That's all, says Jarrah.
*Karri's window's open. Did he go with you
last night? We'll make a map and track him.
You can help.*

She thinks, then shakes her head.
– He didn't come. I went out on my own. He's useless.
Margie, shaking, wants to slap her—
Jarrah holds a hand towards her—*steady, see?
she's listening.*
Margie wants to rage or fly, a feathered thing
released from mothering—but doesn't move.
Watches Jarrah calm their daughter, while their son...
she counts her breaths and forces back the fear.

*– Good. That's useful. Was he in his room
when you went out?*
– I think so.
– What time did you leave?
– 9.24 p.m.
– Good girl. And when did you get back?
– 11.29.
– And was he in his room? Think, honey.
Bat Girl thinks.
Come on now. Look up at his window—is it open?
Bat Girl scrolls back through the night
each mental image clear, time-coded—
finds the frame, expands it

sees the curtains flapping.
Zooms her mind in, looks inside
and sees her brother's empty bed.
– *He wasn't there.*
– *So some time after you went out, he followed?*
– *Must have. Didn't see him. Didn't tell him I was going.*

Conversation over.
Jarrah barrels out to find his son.

Every cell in Margie howls to join him
but she's chained to Bat Girl—who knows what she'd do
left home alone? And they have a system.
Rules and repercussions. *Robot training.*
Bitter thought. She quashes it.
That's a road she mustn't venture down.

Bat Girl: – *Can I go to sleep now?*
– *No!*—her mother, sharp and fraught.
It's time to eat. And then we're going out to K-Mart.
– *Nooooo!* howls Bat Girl.

Bat Girl's chest hurts, burning in the sudden wake
her father left. And Karri—
something in her stomach turns.
My brother's lost.

She hates these seasick body waves.
Can't decode them.
Knows they're caused by people
so she rocks, to drown them out
and drags her mind by willpower
to her dreamed-of caves, where she can think
in silence. Only one more day
till her transmitter maps them out.
And then she'll run away, and...

– Get up. Now, says Margie.
Breakfast. Shower. Shopping.

Misery. The day will drown her—clanging things
and voices, flashing lights, and people.
People. Staring, sweating, chatting in the aisles
with shopping trolleys piled like rattling trucks
with polyester clothes and garish tins of stuff
that clatter loudly at the checkout.
And Bat Girl's head will throb, she'll scowl
and all day long the world will stab
demanding smiles she can't supply.
Margie's knuckles will turn white as well
as violently she steers their cart through K-Mart hell.
The day's a punishment for Margie too
—irrational, she knows—
for failure measured in her daughter.
Public shame offsets her own.
The sideways glances, judgements masked as pity.
Humiliation down the aisles of K-Mart.

Bat Girl doesn't grasp why she's in trouble
—Karri didn't figure in her plans, so not her fault—
it's just one more bewildering event
the world imposes. Worst of all
the timing's awful—only one more day
till the eclipse, when everything lines up.
And so much work to do by then!
TV. Soldering. Tin bear. Wiring—

Bat Girl grinds her teeth, deciding
superhuman good behaviour is the only way
to win the time she needs.

— What do we need at K-Mart, Mum? she asks
and, though her jaw feels rusty, smiles
and looks her startled mother in the eye.

By the creek behind the house
lie Karri's muddy footprints, slowly filling.
Clear at first—the toes dug in
but here they stop, and turn and lose their shape
each stamping out the other.
Which way? They dither, then decide and disappear.
A mossy log bears bruises from his feet.
It lies across the creek then leads to untamed bush—
a tangled mess of hills and bracken
rivulets and boggy patches
left alone—too hard to log.

Jarrah follows, though the log submerges
from his weight, and slides him off.
His boots fill up with water.
Barely stops to empty them
then sets off at a jog through lashing bush.
He has a torch and ropes, and water, compass
blanket too—the boy could have exposure—
even in the summer, nights are cool.

Jarrah's blood is singing in his ears
and jogging's soothing, rhythmic.
Can't hold a thought that freezes, if you're moving.
Doing something. Sun is slanting, afternoon.
The trees lash at his face, blackberry whips
but Jarrah feels no pain, nor will
until he finds his son.

Back at the house, the trip to K–Mart goes awry.
They get as far as seatbelts,
but when Margie backs the Holden out
(too fast) she hits their fence post.
Dings the car and rattles teeth.
Shocked, they sit in silence for a moment
then at the same second, Margie weeps
and Bat Girl laughs
in gulping hoots. The car shakes.
Margie cries so hard that Bat Girl steadies
reaches out and pats her hair
as if it were a doll's. And Margie stops
surprised. A silence full of questions
fills the car. *What now?*

– *Come on, love*, says Margie.
Let's not deal with K-Mart. Let's have lunch.
– *Good idea*, says Bat Girl, eyeing Margie
like a horse that might be bridled
if it gets too close
but wants the sugar in the human hand.
Margie tries a smile. Her daughter grins.
– *You don't like shopping either, Mum!*
Amazed to find this out.
– *No shit*, says Margie.
– *Oooh, you swore!* Now Bat Girl's really laughing
Margie too, in helpless waves
that teeter on the edge of tears.
They leave the car, and shopping bags
and Margie leaves her plans for doing better
integrating Bat Girl, making progress
in the boot. It's just too hard today.
In fact—
she squats down on the porch and rolls a smoke.
– *You hungry, love? I can't be bothered getting lunch.*
– *Not really.* Bat Girl hovers—usually she'd bolt

but something's come undone in Margie
some tight string she ties to Bat Girl
made of pain and punishment
and effort.
Bat Girl wavers, then
sits down herself.

They settle on the porch.
Watch the perfect smoke-rings Margie forms
like kisses, slowly stretch
and break
and disappear.

The afternoon grows ripe, then rotten.
Sun is tilting towards the west, the shadows
stretching through the bush.
And Jarrah's getting nowhere.
Karri's footsteps lead up to a hill, then stop—
the ground's dried out to unforgiving stone.

Jarrah's no bushman—handy with his hands,
a builder, good with clearing land
but not with ploughing through the thickets
hunting. From the hill the dizzy bush spreads out
in waves, set off by sun and wind—it's hard
to get your bearings. Seems like something crashed
and galloped through the bush—the trees are bent—
but here the ground is stony, hard to read.
A mammoth could have thundered through
and left no footprints.

Jarrah sucks his teeth, and circles. Suddenly feels shaky—
four hours' searching takes its toll. Settles on a log
and wipes his face. And tries to think, well knowing

panic gets you nowhere. Rolls a smoke and takes a breath.
Surveys the view. *Oh Christ, the sun*—it's nearly set.
Cold fingers clutch his lungs. He stubs his smoke out,
makes a guess—the rumpled trees, twigs broken
might be Karri's route to water—*smart boy,
surely he'd do that*—then sets off at a run.

∞

Bat Girl's in her room, in panic.
Hates herself for wasting time—she tore away
from Margie, half-way through a sentence.
Slanting sun her cue—four hours till the eclipse!
What was I thinking! So much left to do.

The house is quiet—mercy—Margie crumbled
left Bat Girl in peace.
It's all too much—
her daughter's thaw abruptly stopped—
her son and Jarrah in the bush.
The day's as blank as paper, time suspended.

Margie sits beside the window, gazing out
waiting for her man's return, with boy
or not—and nothing she can do.
She stares, unseeing. Huddles in her mind
a bird's nest rimmed with dark. Pre-dawn.
Before the singing starts.

Bat Girl needs the quiet.
Sucks it in like oxygen.
Jangled by the morning's drama
shredding sounds of shouts and tears
the car colliding with the fence post—
even her own laughter hurts her ears.
Human mud-streams jam her sonar.

144

And everything depends on this next step—
aligning overtones to wires
and bat-song to the tritone stars.

The tin bear squeaks. She takes it out. It glows.
Bat Girl strokes its head and feels it purr.
Good, that part's working—sets it down
and carefully unshrouds her old TV.
It doesn't look impressive—battered by the dump
and scratched and dinged in Jarrah's pick-up truck.
A heavy cube—a baleful eye
like half a broken pair of glasses, staring at you
rimmed by plastic, bottle-thick and useless.

Bat Girl dusts it off, then gets out pliers, copper wire
paperclips, coathangers, tourist cave map
rolls of tinfoil, chewing-gum wrappers
(silvered on the outside, soft inside.
The tin bear tried to chew them—had to be removed
and put to watch on top of the TV).
Bat Girl lays supplies out carefully.
Then she begins.
The TV's rabbit-ears antenna plugs in first.
Then wiring—
subtle humming fills the room.
She works by sound from hot to cold
chaotic to the eye, but ordered to the ear.

On and on she works. The afternoon is stretched
then broken. As the dusk creeps in
the tin bear flickers like a black-and-white TV—
a fragile bridge between the daylight
and that moment when you turn the lights on
snapping dusk to dark.

Margie doesn't stir. Curled round
some small remembered thing
that needs her warmth
she doesn't dare.

In the forest, Jarrah finds the creek.
Pushing back on nightfall, trudges on
hears whispers—
glint of fading sun on water
sounds of frogs and little rustles
night world waking up—but still
there's light enough—there must be.
– *Karri!* Calls out. Echoes. Hears the bush respond
with wary quiet. Then the little sounds
return. *A carpet covering his son.*
Wipes his eyes—then, angry at his weakness,
pushes on.

It's nine o'clock. Bat Girl's exhausted—
smudged beneath the eyes, her ears are ringing.
Wiring took her hours but now it's done—
Come nine-fifteen, it's ready to turn on
and then—she'll see.
Her underworld of caves.
Her future home, lit up in black and silver, waiting—
mapped in phosphorescent swirls on the TV.

Her stomach growling bothers her—
its rumble clashes with the thrumming sound of stars.
And once the bats come—
Bat Girl hasn't eaten since this morning.
Her luck's amazing—usually she has to.

Today, by magic, all the rules are moot.
But damn her stomach!
Bat Girl barrels down to grab some bread and cheese
but then—
she feels a figure swaying.
Turns.
It's Margie.
Standing in the kitchen, staring straight ahead.
Bat Girl waits—but no reaction—
Margie's mind has fled. Bat Girl listens—
pain stirs in her chest—
her mother's thoughts retreat to birds.
Her daughter's not enough.

Bat Girls hears the sound of birds tap-tapping
embryonic in the shell
and feels her mother's mind in flight
retreating into birdsong, light and soft.
And simple tasks—to sing the day.
To warm the shells of creatures made to fly.

Bat Girl feels her mother's buried longing—
fears this new capacity she has
to sense what others feel—
it started with the bear, but now
it's leaking out to others.

She frowns, and pushes what she's sensed aside—
she needs her total focus for the night.

She's brave. But even Bat Girl
focused as she is, takes pause upon the stairs.
Sensing change is waiting in the wings
for her command. Feels the house's pulse—
the muddled streams of Margie, Jarrah, Karri—
everything she fights is all she's known.

Well…*time to go.* She edges in her door.
It isn't easy.
Nests of wires fill the space
like mad macramé, dropped by giants
then thrown against a wall.
It's hard to see the pattern in the woven web,
the squat TV the spider at its center.
The tin bear sits atop—the switch
just waiting for the final wire. Its paw's outstretched
(the rusty shoulder helps to keep its arm up)
Waiting to connect with soldier-like attention.

Bat Girl wiggles through
lifts the jumper leads she filched from Jarrah's truck
and waits.
A thrumming silence fills the house.
A minute…
thirty seconds…
now the edge of moon grows dark
earth's shadow swinging past.
Here come the bats—
a screeching roar of wings and squeaks, unleashed
by star-blasts past the moon—
its dampening effect eclipsed.
Their sonar power will charge the old TV
connect it to the singing stars
and then…

She takes a breath.
And in the dark feels tin bear's eyes find hers.
It's scared.
She sends it thoughts of wings.
Then breathes out hard
And clips its paw to wire.

∞

Way out in the forest Jarrah slumps, defeated.
Dark of moon is absolute—
eclipsed by earth—and treetops hide the stars.
Can't go home without his boy—can't find him.
Tiredness wipes his mind of plans.
The little sounds of night brush past his cheek
and in the darkness, Jarrah comes undone
at first unmoving, like an ice cube melting
then in shuddered stifled weeping.

Karri missing, Bat Girl's storms and Margie's fading smile—
the whole misguided move to Witchcliffe.
What a ship of fools they were, self-quarantined
away from town, with nothing to sustain them
but subtraction. All of it his fault.
He let it happen.

Jarrah stands, and calls again. No answer comes.
He sinks down on his knees and begs
and makes a silent bargain with his son.

Back in Bat Girl's room, the wires connect.
A searing flash of light streaks through the room.
The air ignites. The TV switches on.
The tin bear glows red hot
then burns to white. A humming starts
then builds to screeching, shaking walls.
Oh no! A feedback loop!
She hadn't planned for this. She howls.

A ripping pain tears through her head like summer
    lightning.
And it doesn't stop.

The echo chamber's filling up
with waves that build and crest and break
and shatter something in her head. She falls
and feels her wires uncoil
go snaking out, flash through the walls
and disappear into the silver night.

She's done it.

For just one moment, everything lights up
above and under earth.
Karri, in the forest, hidden by the river
Margie, in the light-struck house
Bat Girl, clutching ears and howling
neighbours troubled by a sudden storm—
the sky awash with bats, not rain.

Every creek and rock burns silver
etched in sharpest light.
The secret caves below pulsate
their lake-filled shadowy dark shapes revealed.
Translucent earth. The trees
are swaying ghosts, a smudge of light
turned into leaves and bark—and creatures
brief as sparks—so hard to catch—
just shimmers on the surface
scarcely shadows.

Back out in the bush, the creek flames silver.
Must be summer lightning—Jarrah turns—
and in the brilliance crackling through the sky
sees Karri's jacket. Soft blue cloth hung on a branch
torn off in speed. The kid has made a trail
a metre wide—he's skidded through the forest

clutching branches, tearing up young trees.
Then suddenly, the light is gone.
But Jarrah laughs—a sort of howl—
he's seen enough to run towards his son.

He jumps a log, then turns—just metres on
from where he'd sat, lies Karri. Eyes closed.
Pale, but breathing. Skin is chilled
a huge lump on his forehead. Jarrah falls.
When Karri stirs and mumbles, *Dad?*
he slings him up across his back
and heads home at a gallop.

AUNTIE

Far away in Perth, when Bat Girl's wires connect
the evening flickers, like a candle going out
—you'd blink and miss it—
Auntie shivers in the back seat of the bus.
Glimpses Sally Jo for five bright seconds—
blazing through the dark like lightning
sealed in light and very far away.
Sally laughing in a waterfall—
or nightclub? Somewhere silver
she's a flash of swirling limbs and hair
behind a roaring shimmer-wall of white—
showing off, she's dancing on the edge
where water turns to diamond light and breaks.

Cloudy ropes of vapour rise around her
ghosting the ravines behind the waterfall—
or is it just the fog-machine that's weaving steamy loops
between the dancers and the mirror ball?
Auntie can't be sure. The background flickers
—*nightclub, waterfall*—
around the incandescent, laughing girl.

Sally howls aloud as light breaks round her.
Water—or the throb of bass?— pounds on her head
half-ecstasy, half-terror, washing out the past.
She laughs and spins—she's waving to her friends.

She's done it.
Broken through that roaring wall of white.

Sally turns towards her friends, away from Auntie—
shaking her black curls, her arms stretched high
bathed in applause, she steps towards a shining curtain
flanked by men in suits with hard dark stares.
Some kind of act? She's dancing in a club—

but, stranger than her silvered skin, or fog machine
or dancing rainbows from the mirror ball—
her friends are white kids. Where's she gone?
The men nod—let her through, new friends in tow.

And then she's gone.
And then the light shuts off.

Auntie's shaking in her seat.
Knows she won't find Sally now—
she's gone beyond the world they share
wherever else she is.
She's cut the cord of blood, and gone.

The bus seems drained of colour
now the sun's gone down
recycling dirty greens and greys
that flicker in the dim fluorescent light.
It's that empty time of day—the stretch
before the night unfolds, when those that can
go home and unpack groceries
start the dinner, shrug their worker's skin off
settle in. And those that can't
glance past the others' well-lit windows
towards the alleyways and parks
scouting out a temporary home
to shelter in the dark.

Hold on a few more stops. Swap when the driver does—
Then cross the road, switch buses...
Survival mode. Her brain is clamping down.
Auntie shrinks inside the bus's metal skin
like dried-up desert seed between the rains.

BAT GIRL

Light blasts Margie's eyeballs.
And that sound—a thrumming roar—
She's running up the stairs before she's formed a thought—
disaster on a scale of ten can only be her daughter.

Bat Girl's door is open.
Margie, stunned, stands at the threshold.
Blackened wires fill the room—
some writhe like angry snakes.
A cloud of bats, suspended at the window
hovers in the air like humming birds
who've scented nectar, poised to dive.

A luminous blue light pulsates from the TV
and on the screen
a jerky sequence plays.
Tin-suited insects leap
out of a spaceship
to the moon.
They crouch, then—
such slow motion—
jump.
No dust.
They land and bend their knees and leap again.
And then, suspended in mid-leap
the TV loops.
And on.
Around it goes.
As if there's rust in space.

The astronauts' slow motion fills the room
and turns her bones to water.
Slowly Margie turns—
it takes an aeon—finding Bat Girl by the bed
curled in a corner.

Bat Girl never cries, but now—
clutched in her hand, a battered toy
a metal bear, quite small.
It's rusty—looks like Bat Girl found it in a ditch
half full of water, after some kid dropped it.
The toy's rust stains her hands.
It looks like blood
(the old kind, once it's dried).

Margie's heart cracks. Bends down
whispers – *What's the matter?* to her daughter.
Bat Girl looks at her—right in the eye, how strange—
– *I broke him. Didn't mean to. It's my fault*
and clutches harder
clinging fiercely to her metal toy.

Dread floods Margie.
Karri—what has Bat Girl done?
But then the door downstairs bangs open.
Margie turns and runs downstairs
to find her husband carrying their son.

It took a week to clean out Bat Girl's room.
The kids slept through the worst of that—
they both crawled out to eat
then back to bed.

Bat Girl needed Valium
before her hand unclenched enough
to take the tin bear out.
Even drugged, she'd shake her head,
like a swimmer trying to clear her ears
of water. Falling over—dizzy days—
she'd lost her balance.

Says she's lost her hearing
but to Margie, Bat Girl seems to hear much more.
Answers questions—stops herself and scowls
annoyed to understand the mud stream.

Karri got away with X-rays
and a bandage on his knee.

The bats have gone.
Once Jarrah took an axe to that TV
(it spooked them out, those astronauts
stuck out in space) the bats dispersed.
The humming stopped. The lights came on
and Bat Girl's black-snake wires lay calm.

The house is full of careful silence
like a beach still strewn with wreckage
after a giant wave recedes.
The weather's calm
but trust in the horizon's gone—
everyone keeps glancing out to sea.

∞

A strange hiatus settles in. The days crawl past.
It's hot—the summer's hanging on.
The bush is full of wicked thorns and weeds.
Bat Girl walks, and swishes flies.
She scowls and kicks a rock—she hates the sun
but night's become opaque—
a sonar soup she can't swim through.

Bat Girl misses water singing underground
the tritone shrill of stars, the sonar web of bats.
She feels them pulse
but nothing sounds the same—

she can't quite bring them in—
the world ensnares instead.
She's trapped in some strange limbo
between the world of bats and people.

She scowls again and kicks another rock.
It ricochets, and plummets—
good, she's nearly there—
and then the wild bush tangle stops.
And here's the sea.
She climbs the boulder at the cliff's edge.
Before her, limestone cliffs fall sheer to sea.
Behind her, tangled bush.
Above are screeching gulls.
The wind whips. Birds shriek. Surf thuds.
Sky and water, rocks and sun—
cacophony of everything and nothing.

Bat Girl shuts her eyes
and lets the bedlam of the world in.
The salt wind roars inside her wounded ears
and in the bone-bound echo chamber of her head
swirls round the ashy hole the tin bear left.

She huddles on the rock and howls
protected by the louder howling of the world.
She sits there till the wind dies down
then every day at sunset heads for home.

Till one day, on the path home
Bat Girl overhears her brother slashing weeds.

Bat Girl watches, out of sight.
The stick he's swinging breaks.
He shouts and hurls it in the bush.
He spits. His hands are scored with red.

Bat Girl waits. When Karri yells
and kicks a stump, then runs
she feels his rage beat through her blood.

How strange to hear
as if her brother were a bat, or star.
Humans are a murky swamp
but *Karri's stick?* That could be interesting.
A way to flatten growing things...
That dull thwack-thwack of Karri's—
it didn't match the task.
Surely there's a better tool...

She ponders it, her eyes half-closed
the trees still rippling in her brother's wake.
The wind dies down.
The dusk pools, silent, near the trees.
Then something stirs—
so soft, you'd barely hear it—
brushing sound of skin on brittle leaves
a glint of silver-black—*a snake!*—
it's suddenly between her feet—
it slithers through and vanishes
inside a hollow log.

She startles—shakes—belatedly afraid.
She wipes her sweaty palms
and counts her breaths until they slow
one...two...three...four...
A small breeze stirs the leaves, dies down.
The trees are silhouettes now
black on cobalt blue.
Bat Girl doesn't move—
but then she smiles.
Now there's a thought...

Bat Girl comes home late. Runs in
a salt-stained, bush-whipped mess.
— *You dropped this*—to her brother
shoves at him the broken stick
he slashed the bushes with.
His face burns. *Is she mocking him?*
— *It doesn't work*, says Bat Girl.
Dad, I need some wire. Dad?
— *Not now*, says Jarrah sharply, eyes on Karri.
— *Later?*
— *Maybe.*
— *What does that mean?*
— *Beatrice*, Margie snaps, *just go to bed.*
— *All right!* And Bat Girl stomps upstairs.

— *So what was that?* says Karri.
Then, much louder, *What?! I hate her.*
Silence boils and simmers.
Margie bites the insides of her cheeks.
Nobody breathes. Then—
— *Guess what, kid.* That's Jarrah.
Karri's surly — *What?*
— *I'm headed up to Perth next week.*
New contract on a house.
You wanna come? Just you and me.
You help out mornings on the job—
I'll drop you at the pool for afternoons.

Karri doesn't answer. Can't.
As if a rock he'd pushed uphill for years
had rolled away, and left him stupid,
empty-handed. — *Go to bed*, says Margie, gently.
Karri runs upstairs and slams the door.

The house vibrates.
It takes a moment, like a ruffled cat.

But then it settles down
and slowly falls asleep.
Margie and Jarrah wait
till Karri's light is out
then head outside—the night is thick with stars.

In the darkness, Karri stares straight up
turns over Jarrah's words—*just you and me.*
Feels the prison doors of night unlatch
the subtle turning of the earth
for too long stuck in place—
and as his eyes fall shut the road to Perth lights up.

Pool dreams.
Dazzling sun on water.
Green-glass Jackie.

In the attic room above him, Bat Girl ponders.
Karri's stick will never work.
But something to snake out a path
and flatten all those stinging weeds
for daylight walks—*that could be useful*
especially now her hearing's changed—
the night's slammed shut
and taken with it all her dreams of caves.
She needs a new device—the kind
that weeds will hear, and bend before.
Perhaps cicada casings with the legs intact
to rub their violin-string shiver sounds.
And tin works well—she has some rusty tins...

The night curves on as Bat Girl works.
She follows a new hunch—her last machine
was crude, too all-or-nothing—
Locked to energies its circuits couldn't hold.
This time, she'll tap the power of the small

like cicadas do, all shrilling in a field
until it turns to aural glass
and shatter-shimmers in your ear.

And now she has the shape—*a snake!*
She makes a spine of wire the length of Karri's stick—
he almost got it right—it's portable for walks—
but hers will flex. She'll take a skin that bends
then fill it in, and seal it shut with glue.
She needs some fragile creature-parts
that marry bone to wind
and let the air sing through her skin
but where's she stashed them…?

Bat Girl thinks. Then tenses.
Rusty wire constricts her lungs.
The things she needs are in the tin bear's drawer.
She hasn't touched it since that night—
she'd shoved the bear inside
wrapped in an old black T-shirt—
slammed it shut to deal with later.
Bat Girl shuts her eyes and breathes
then pulls it open, takes the bear out.

Somehow it looks smaller—
less a creature, more a thing—
rusted, dinged, less shiny.
One tinfoil ear has fallen off.
The button eyes are blank.

She opens up the window
—*simple, now there's no alarm*—
and lays it on the window ledge outside.
Turns, but then—it's odd.
She ought to say—but what?
Sweet dreams, she mutters.

That's what Margie says each night.
Meaningless, but part of bedtime.

Bat Girl clicks the window shut—*that's that*—
and opens up the drawer again.
A shiver of excitement. *New machine!*
She takes out rows of bat skulls, tissue thin
threads them carefully to copper wire
then lays them out along a snake's discarded skin.

Margie and Jarrah sit on the porch
and watch the stars. They mean to talk
but somehow words dry up.
They're strangely shy
like people who survived a landslide
(clutching naked at each other)
meeting later at a dinner party.

Crescent moon.
The land's asleep again
its secret caves in darkness far below
sealed up from view, away from mortal eyes.
The bush is full of little sounds.
The creek flows on, its quiet murmur unperturbed
by the bat-wing flickers of their human lives.

JEROME

The tin bear, scarred by fire and rust
waits on the ledge outside the window.
The shiny metal sparkles in the sun
a magpie swoops in low
—its wings beat on the window—
snatches up the pretty thing, and goes.

The forest spirals down as up they fly.
They circle over sea, then skyward.
Bright air strokes the tin bear's face
and tickles, like the mouse's whiskers in the cot
—*Wake up. Wake up.*

Jerome the moon-bear laughs, and wakes
from some strange dream of bats and stars
and scowling dark-brown eyes
and blazing lights and wires—
it slides away before it turns to story.

Now—*where am I?* Pictures start to form.
He's been this way before, but in reverse.
For here's the blazing grid of Perth.
All hard and shiny.
Roads and roaring buses, forest gone.
The rows of houses cling like pigweed to the sandy soil.

He wants to fly away, but something draws him
down towards the swimming pool where Sally flew—
the house, the baking road where Darryl danced
on silver skates, defying raging cars
and then the big green bus came. Then...

Bird and metal bear survey the scene
as if there's something missing, some last clue
to make time move again.

But nothing moves
but them.
And in a flash, the moon-bear knows—
it never will—
it's circle endlessly, or go.

He tugs, but some dark cord resists
a heavy tether, hidden. *What?*
Words chase shadows, darkening the sky—
Auntie, Sally Jo—they're calling him to earth.
That's it! His name's the leash.
Goodbye, Jerome. He wriggles free.
The bird drops bear—a flashing silver thing—
banks through sudden clouds
ascends, is gone.

Far from the blazing light of Perth
adrift in silky tropic twilight, Sally sways.
Her eyes are closed—
she's lost inside a song—
so when someone in the band shouts
– *Hey, look up! A shooting star!*
she glances up too late. It's gone.

The tin bear's falling shakes the earth
like wind shakes grass—
a shiver in the eye, lost in a blink.
But Auntie, circling on the bus, sits up.
She knows. The boy's gone home.

She shuts her eyes.

Soon, no doubt, they'll find the body he's shrugged off
in some grey no-man's-land, released
from where it snagged beneath some truck.

She stares out of the window into dusk.
The last pink light is fading from the sky—
the dark creeps up here from the ground—
the sky holds on.

And in the window, as the dark congeals
her own reflection hems her in—
her eyes are blackened holes.
She gazes through them into nothing
barely breathing
blinking with the motion of the bus.

But in the bleakness, something shifts
behind the flatness of the glass
and other eyes stare through her own.
And other eyes behind—
She breathes in sharply. Here they are—
the boy, then Sally's dad, and farther back
in glinting flashes, glimpsed behind them both
her own lost mother's.
Soft black eyes, like Auntie's.

And she's smiling
trying to tell her—*what?*—
the face is melting
leaves her with a whisper—
home...

Auntie squints her eyes and rocks
in quiet rhythm with the bus.
She's not asleep
but can't quite wake up yet.
She gathers strength.
Five stops. Five more—
She pulls the cord, and finally gets off.

Tonight, she'll get her ticket back to Geraldton.
Time for family.
Tell what's happened.
Time to take tomorrow's Greyhound home.

CODA: SALLY JO

Twenty years later
Perth's awash with mining cash.
Flash new houses sell for millions—
fly-in fly-out homes for miners.
A place to park the wife and kids, who wait
to see the men on rostered five-day leave
(too short—too long)
between their fortnight shifts up north.

In Leederville these days
there's fewer purple cars with screaming tyres
and fights on Friday nights
and broken windows up above the pool halls.
These days, you can have dinner in a dozen places.
Indian, Sri Lankan and of course Chinese.
And cafés, some with ice-cream, line the block
down from the independent movie house.

In Leederville these days, it isn't hard to find a spot
to sip a coffee, watch the world go by.
The men in linen shirts tucked into jeans
the girls in strappy sandals
and those pretty cotton frocks.

The elegant woman lingers in the café
gazes out the window
makes some mental notes.
She'll order some pashminas for next season
And maybe some fine cotton shirts—
looks like Indian cotton's made a comeback.
Doodles on her napkin—they'd look good in prints.
Indian cotton, Yamatji designs—
she'll check the latest works from Geraldton.
These days, Indigenous art is hot.

She scans the list of painters in her mind—
They'd sell like hotcakes in her trendy Freo shop.

Something bright—black, orange, silver—
That bush tucker series? No, too subtle.
Maybe those new magpie paintings.
But on shirts? Too garish.
Perfect for the scarves and skirts.

She can't sit here forever though. It's time.

And so she drains her coffee, leaves the change
and heads up Vincent Street.

It takes a while—it's further than it looks.
Uphill. But Beatty Park's unmissable.
A shabby blue behemoth
all washed up among the cracks and weeds.
There's yellow tape around the concrete stairs—
Spray-painted signs too hopefully announce
Closed for Repairs.

She pauses at the traffic lights.
They change, then change again.
The roaring waves of cars wash by
and still she waits.

Across the road, another woman stands.
If you squinted, you might think them twins—
curly dark hair, slender, in their thirties—
but the moment passes.
The other woman's flanked by toddlers
anchored to her stroller by their sticky hands.
She bends towards them.
Then for a moment, glances up to Beatty Park.
Sees again the silver arc she blazed

through summer air
back in the day...

Her littlest breaks her reverie.

Jackie roughly grabs his shirt
to stop him dashing into traffic—
Crosses with the lights
then heads on down the hill.

The elegant woman watches till they're gone.

She checks her watch.
And then her hair.
Spins around—
was that a rustle in the grass?
but no-one's there.
The pool's shut, after all
and the houses all have walls these days
to shield them from the roaring cars.

It takes a while. She finds the spot.
A grassy dimple shaded by a ghost gum
edged by fallen leaves and peeled-off bark
behind the concrete shelter of the bus stop.

Sally Jo bends down, unties her hair
and in the long breath between the waves of cars
lays down her scarlet scrunchie
and a new tin bear.

She's done it.
There. It isn't much.
And now—
she stands.

A silver cloud forms over Beatty Park
this cloudless summer day.
The elegant woman cries behind her glasses
whispers something
tucks her hair behind her ear.
She wants to stay—but here's the bus
(it's Kevin's Friday shift)
so on she gets.

And pretty soon the wind comes up
and blows the cloud away.

ACKNOWLEDGEMENTS

For various combinations of sustenance, critical comment, advice, friendship and cheering on:

Rosemary Ahern; Claire Chafee; Rachel Crawford; Wesley Enoch; Gail Evans; Jenny Evans; Pat and Ernie Evans; Jennifer Natalya Fink; Gráinne Fox; Derek Goldman; Louise Gough; Mireille Juchau; Elizabeth Lane; Liane Lang; Holly Laws; Nadia Mahdi; Charlotte Meehan; Joseph Megel; Wendy Revell; Maya Roth; Beth Spencer; Mary-Lou Stephens; Lian Tanner; Kathleen Tolan; Katherine Vaz; Ciella Williams; Josephine Wilson and Ann Woodhead: Thank you all so much. Additional thanks to Rosalba Clemente for inspiration, hospitality and kindness.

My deep gratitude to Erik Ehn and to the Flea Theater's Pataphysics program, run by Anne Washburn and Gary Winter, for the silent writing retreat at Eagle Nest Ranch in Texas. The heat, green river and limestone cliffs evoked long-ago Perth summers and inspired this tale.

I'm thankful to Tammy Greenwood, who provided vital editorial comment on the first draft; to Peter Matheson, whose inspired insight and tough love helped shape the next two, and to Nicola Redhouse, who edited the publication draft.

Thanks to Carole Sargent, and the Office of Scholarly Publications at Georgetown University which she directs, for invaluable advice and camaraderie; likewise to the Writers Room DC.

I'm grateful to The Corporation of Yaddo and the Bogliasco Foundation for the gifts of time and space, and to the Australia Council for the Arts for assistance with residency travel costs.

My sincere thanks to Terri-ann White, Kate Pickard, Charlotte Guest and the great team at UWA Publishing.

And finally, my love and thanks to Rick Massimo, for everything else.

Printed in Australia
AUOC02n0658180815
269678AU00006B/8/P